RAYMOND & GRAHAM

BASES LOADED

BY **Mike Knudson**

ILLUSTRATED BY **Stacy Curtis**

VIKING
An Imprint of Penguin Group (USA) Inc.

VIKING
Published by Penguin Group
Penguin Young Readers Group, 345 Hudson Street, New York, New York 10014, U.S.A.
Penguin Group (Canada), 90 Eglinton Avenue East, Suite 700, Toronto, Ontario, Canada M4P 2Y3
(a division of Pearson Penguin Canada Inc.)
Penguin Books Ltd, 80 Strand, London WC2R 0RL, England
Penguin Ireland, 25 St Stephen's Green, Dublin 2, Ireland (a division of Penguin Books Ltd)
Penguin Group (Australia), 250 Camberwell Road, Camberwell, Victoria 3124, Australia
(a division of Pearson Australia Group Pty Ltd)
Penguin Books India Pvt Ltd, 11 Community Centre, Panchsheel Park, New Delhi – 110 017, India
Penguin Group (NZ), 67 Apollo Drive, Rosedale, North Shore 0745, Auckland, New Zealand
(a division of Pearson New Zealand Ltd.)
Penguin Books (South Africa) (Pty) Ltd, 24 Sturdee Avenue, Rosebank, Johannesburg 2196, South Africa

Penguin Books Ltd, Registered Offices: 80 Strand, London WC2R 0RL, England

First published in 2009 by Viking, a division of Penguin Young Readers Group

1 3 5 7 9 10 8 6 4 2

Text copyright © Mike Knudson, 2009
Illustrations copyright © Stacy Curtis, 2009
All rights reserved

LIBRARY OF CONGRESS CATALOGING-IN-PUBLICATION DATA
Knudson, Mike.
Raymond and Graham : bases loaded / by Mike Knudson ; illustrated by Stacy Curtis.
p. cm.
Summary: Fourth grade best friends Raymond and Graham try to avoid the class bully, have fun with a
substitute teacher, and get the attention of the girls they like while concentrating on winning the Little League
Championships.
ISBN 978-0-670-01205-3 (hardcover)
[1. Baseball—Fiction. 2. Schools—Fiction. 3. Best friends—Fiction. 4. Friendship—Fiction.
5. Mothers and sons—Fiction.] I. Curtis, Stacy, ill. II. Title. III. Title: Bases loaded.
PZ7.K7836Ram 2010
[Fic]—dc22
2009015199

Manufactured in China   Set in Chaparral Pro   Book design by Jim Hoover

For Annette, the best teammate ever
—M.K.

For Bram and Rory,
fellow Kane County Cougars fans —S.C.

Prologue

IT HAD BEEN almost nine months since last year's championship baseball game, but that day still haunted me. Striking out in the first inning, sitting on a wad of gum, and having my mom walk right into the dugout to give me a big kiss for good luck in front of both teams, the parents, the umpires, the snack bar workers . . . everyone. It was humiliating.

But this year was going to be different. I could feel it in my bones, I could smell it in the air— I could even taste it. This wasn't going to be just another year of making it to the finals and then blowing it. This would be the year of winning it all. That's right, I'm talking about the year we would earn the title of Millcreek Little League Champions!

Batter Up

THE UMPIRE PULLED the mask from the top of his head onto his face and wiggled it around until it fit just right. *"Batter up!"* I slowly walked to the plate, enjoying the moment of my first time up to bat this season.

Things were already looking better than last year. It was a warm Saturday morning in April. The grass seemed greener, the sun seemed brighter, and most important, it was opening day and my mom wasn't here. She had to take Grandma to the doctor. Don't get me wrong, it's not that I don't like my mom coming to my games. My mom's great. It's just that this was the first game since last year's good-luck kiss disaster, and I wanted to make sure it went smoothly and nothing embarrassing happened. My dad was in the stands, but he usually didn't cause too much trouble. He might argue with the umpire now and then or maybe with a parent from the other team, but that's just part of baseball. Plus, he doesn't really get mad when he argues. He just likes to get in the last word no matter what.

Dad had also dragged my thirteen-year-old sister, Geri, to the game. She looked bored as usual. I could tell she didn't want to be there. But that didn't bother me. In fact, it just made the day seem even better. It was like my own little way of getting back at her for always being so mean, without her even knowing.

There was only one slight problem: we were playing the Pirates, and David Miller was pitching that day. Not only is he the biggest, meanest kid our age, but he's also the fastest pitcher in the league. I don't want to brag, but I'm one of the best batters on our team. I can hit off almost anyone. But there's just something different about David. Maybe it's the nasty things he says to me when I walk up to the plate or that crazy laugh of his. For some reason I always play terribly against him. That's another reason I didn't want Mom here. There was no way I could handle my mom being embarrassing and David being mean in the same game.

Finally, I made it to the plate. I tapped my bat against my cleats and then dug my back foot into the dirt. After a few practice swings, I held the bat back and waited for the pitch. Without even one mean comment, David started his windup and threw the ball.

The ball barely missed my head! Luckily, I'd dropped to the ground in time.

"Ball!" yelled the ump.

David just stood there laughing his crazy laugh. I got up and dusted off my pants. I was shaking all over.

"Good eye," Coach Parker called from over by first base. He scratched his chin through his big, bushy, black beard.

Good eye? I thought. *I was just trying to save myself from getting hit in the face.* I looked over at Coach. He smiled. He's been my coach since I played T-ball and knows me pretty well. He's Kevin's dad, but even Kevin calls him Coach. He knows everything about baseball. Plus, things like almost getting hit in the face don't bother him. He just says stuff like, "Brush it off and get back in there." Kevin says that back in high school his dad was the star of the team. Even though the other coaches just wear a T-shirt with their teams' logo on it, Coach Parker always wears a full uniform, down to the cleats.

I took a few more practice swings and was ready for the second pitch. I could hear my teammates cheering. Carlos's parents were screaming something in Spanish to me. They always screamed in Spanish to Carlos when he was up to bat. It seemed to work for him. He was one of our better hitters.

David smiled at me. "Hey, what's the matter?" he said. "Don't have your mommy here to give you a good-luck kiss?" His whole team started laughing. Even some of my teammates laughed.

All right, I said to myself. *This is it! I'm going to hit this ball so hard David will never make fun of me again.* I gripped the bat tighter and stared back at David with the meanest face I could make.

"Oooh, scary," David said. Then he threw the second pitch. Again I fell to the ground as the ball came right at me. Unfortunately, as I fell, the ball hit my bat by accident and bounced into the backstop.

"Foul ball! Strike one!" the ump called.

"What do you mean, strike one?" I yelled from the ground. "I didn't even swing. Besides, he almost killed me!"

"The ball touched your bat. That's a foul ball," the ump said, getting back down in his squatting position behind the catcher and adjusting his mask.

"Hang in there, Raymond," Coach said. "You're a hitter. Be patient."

"That stinks," I said under my breath, waiting for the next pitch.

As David threw the third pitch I jumped out of the way quickly and lowered my bat so I wouldn't accidentally hit the ball again. Only this time, the ball flew right across the plate.

"Strike two!"

David was laughing harder than ever. "Got you scared."

He was right—now I was completely nervous. Was he going to try to hit me again, would he throw a strike, or what? I stared at David and concentrated on the ball. As he was winding up I saw a smile stretch out across his face. *He's smiling because he's going to throw it at me,* I decided. Then, just as the ball left his hand, I thought, *Maybe he's smiling because he's throwing a strike and thinks I'm going to jump out of the way again.* Before I knew it the umpire had yelled, "Strike three, batter's out!" I didn't even swing.

I walked back to the dugout humiliated, dragging my bat on the ground. Everyone told me "good try" and "you'll get 'em next time" and all those other things you say when someone strikes out.

"Looked like a ball to me," Dad called out to the umpire. Next to him, Geri rolled her eyes.

"Not even close," came a reply from a mom on the other team. It was Brian's mom. Dad looked over at her.

"It should have been a ball," Dad answered.

"Good call, ump," Brian's mom said. She stared over at my dad.

"Not a good call." Dad said it softly, but just loud enough to be heard. Brian's mom shook her head and turned back to the game.

There are six teams in our league. Most of the players go to East Millcreek Elementary, like me, and Upland Terrace Elementary. The East Millcreek kids are split up among three teams: the Giants, the Pirates, and a few on the Tigers. Luckily, Graham and I are both on the Giants.

Even though we play against all five other teams, David's team is always our biggest rival. Some years we do better than the Pirates, and other years, like last year, they do better than we do. But this year, we were determined to beat them in the Little League Championships. Next year we would hopefully be in the majors, the next league up from Little League. In the majors you get to play with the older kids. The coaches and players of the Major League teams often come by and watch the Little League Championship game looking for the best players to pick for their teams next year.

Ever since we were little first-graders, Graham and I had dreamed of being picked for the best Major League team. Last year the Marlins won the Major League Championship. Graham and I went to the final game. They clobbered the Cardinals 11–2. They were definitely the team we wanted to be on next year.

Graham was up to bat next. David turned toward the outfield. "Easy out—everyone move in closer. He can't hit that far."

Unlike me, Graham loved the trash talk of baseball. He was our catcher, and he always said the same kinds of things to the other team's batters when they were at the plate. So nothing David said bothered him. He just smiled and got ready to swing.

The first pitch came in high for ball one. The second hit the dirt right in front of the plate. "Ball two!" yelled the ump. The third pitch came in straight down the middle. Graham swung as hard as he could and hit the ball. Unfortunately, the ball didn't go too far. It just bounced off his bat and rolled slowly to David, who picked it up with his bare hand and threw Graham out at first base.

The rest of the game went about the same way. Our team really stunk it up. We ended up losing by six runs.

"Great game, bud," Dad said afterward as we headed to the car.

I looked up at him. "What do you mean? We got killed!"

"Right," he answered, trying to think of something good to say about the game. "I was talking about the great hit you had."

"Do you mean the time I fell on the ground and

the ball accidentally hit my bat or the time I swung as hard as I could and missed the ball by a mile?"

"Um, the first one?" Dad said, smiling. Before I could answer he said, "Let's go get some ice cream." That worked for me.

The rest of the weekend, I tried not to think about the game. Coach always says that once the game's over, we should forget about it and start thinking about the next game. But every game is important this year. Only the top two teams get to play in the championship game, and losing our first game wasn't a good sign.

Grandma Gibson

ON MONDAY MORNING Mom drove me to school. She said she had to talk to the secretary about something. It was a nice change from walking. We picked up Graham and got to school early, and he and I hung around on the front steps waiting for the first bell to ring. We talked about the lousy game we had Saturday and how we were going to destroy the Tigers this week. We always had one game during the week and one every Saturday. The Tigers were probably the worst team in the league.

"I think I'm going to invite Kelly to come watch the game tomorrow," Graham said with a big smile on his face. Graham's been in love with Kelly since the first grade. "The Tigers would be a great team to show off against. You should invite Heidi to come watch." I wasn't sure I was ready for that. I mean, I do like Heidi . . . you know, like a girlfriend. And even though I thought she liked me too, I wasn't so sure about inviting her to our game.

"I don't think so," I said. "After that last game, I don't want any distractions. I just want to have a good game and get my confidence back. What if I get all nervous with her at the game and play even worse?"

"I really think you should invite her anyway," Graham said, looking desperate. "I mean, this is the Tigers we're talking about. We're going to look good for sure. Plus, I heard Zach broke his finger after the game on Saturday. So you'll probably be starting pitcher."

"I don't know," I said. "If I invite her, she'll think I like her."

"But you *do* like her. That's the point," Graham said.

"But if I invite her, then she'll know I like her. And I don't want her to know I like her unless I know she likes me first. And even then . . . well . . . I don't know, I can't explain it," I said. I knew Graham wouldn't understand. He has liked Kelly forever and always makes sure she knows it. He tells her all the time.

"Come on, *hermano*," Graham said. "You've got to invite her." I knew he was serious because he was calling me *hermano*. That's "brother" in Spanish, and we only use the few words we know in Spanish when it's really important or on special occasions.

"Well, maybe I'll invite her to a game some other time," I said. "Why do you care so much about whether I invite her?"

"Well, it's just that . . . Kelly would probably come if she knew other girls were going to be there. And I kind of, um . . . well, I kind of got excited about the whole idea and . . ."

"And what, Graham?" I said. He was hiding something. I could tell.

"Okay, don't be mad, but I kind of told Heidi—" Graham started.

"What? You kind of told Heidi what?" I said, grabbing him by his shoulders.

"That you wanted her to come to your next game and that you were going to invite her today," Graham said quickly in a quiet voice. His freckly face was all scrunched up, and he took a step back like I was going to punch him or something.

"WHAT?" I yelled. "Why would you do that? Now what am I supposed to do? I can't *not* ask her, because she'll think that I'm uninviting her and that I don't like her. But if I ask her, she'll think I *do* like her. Oh, man, this is terrible." I dropped my head into my hands. Just then I heard two familiar voices.

"Hi, Raymond. Hi, Graham," they said together. I looked up to see Heidi and Diane standing right in front of me. Diane is Heidi's best friend. She's also the tallest girl in our school. Actually, I think she's taller than all of the boys too, except David. We've all known each other since we were little kids.

"What's wrong with you?" Diane asked.

"Nothing, I was just . . . um . . . resting my head in my hands," I answered, putting my hands down and trying to look normal.

"Hey, Raymond was just saying how he wanted to ask you guys to come to our baseball game tomorrow. Right, Raymond?" Graham jabbed me in the ribs.

"I don't know," Diane said, not looking too interested. "Is the snack bar going to be open?"

"Come on," Graham wheedled. "Where else can you experience quality sporting entertainment like this?"

Diane rolled her eyes. "Right. Watching you strike out is high quality."

"Hey, if I strike out, I'll buy you a candy bar from the snack bar."

"Now you're talking." Diane grinned. "Now I'll definitely be there."

"Hey, do I get something if you guys strike out?" Heidi added.

"Yeah, Graham will buy you a candy bar too," I added quickly. Graham glared at me. We all shook hands on the deal, and the girls went inside.

"See," Graham said, "that wasn't so hard. It worked out perfectly." I wasn't so sure. I didn't want to get too nervous at the game with Heidi watching.

"Come on, *hermano*," Graham said, putting his arm around my shoulder. "You'll thank me later." We walked up the stairs and headed to class.

"So, Raymond, how was your weekend?" David said, plopping down at his desk next to mine. "Nice foul ball you hit as you were falling to the ground. I think that was your best hit of the game."

"I only fell because you were trying to hit me," I said. He was really getting under my skin.

"No, if I were trying to hit you, I would have hit you—like this," he said, giving me a hard slug on the arm.

"David," Mrs. Gibson called out. "Why don't you sit up here by me today?" We all watched as David pushed his desk up by Mrs. Gibson's. I don't think there has been one single week this year when David hasn't had to sit near Mrs. Gibson for at least a day. And it was usually because he got caught hitting me. I wondered why she didn't just permanently move him by some girls or something. I don't think he would hit a girl. Oh well, at least I didn't have to worry about him for the rest of the day.

"All right, students," Mrs. Gibson said, "I have something to tell you." Usually she sits on a stool in front of the class to start the day. But today I could see that whatever she had to tell us was more important than usual. She stood in front of the class with her long, skinny arms folded. She pulled one hand out to adjust her huge glasses but then quickly tucked it back under her other arm. "First of all, please remember that this Friday is picture day. At the end of the day today I will pass out the order forms. Secondly, I will be gone all of next week visiting my daughter and my new granddaughter."

Mrs. Gibson's a grandma? I thought to myself. Of course, I knew that teachers were regular people, but somehow I never thought of her as actually being someone's grandma.

"I am counting on all of you to be on your best behavior and treat our substitute as you would treat me," she continued. "Is that clear to everyone?" Lizzy immediately raised her hand, as she always does when Mrs. Gibson asks a question.

"It's very clear to me, Mrs. Gibson," Lizzy said. "Everything you say is always clear to me."

"Thank you, Lizzy," Mrs. Gibson answered.

"You're welcome, Mrs. Gibson." Lizzy continued, "By the way, can we call you while you're gone if we need to?"

"No, I'm afraid not, Lizzy," Mrs. Gibson answered. "But I'm sure there won't be anything to call me about. Our substitute will be able to handle everything that comes up." Everyone just looked around at each other without saying a thing. Then Mrs. Gibson wrote the spelling words for the week on the board, and the school day continued as usual.

Recess came, and everyone exited the classroom quietly. But as soon as we made it outside, we were all talking about the news. "A substitute!

One whole week with a substitute!" It was the talk of the entire playground.

"This is going to be so sweet!" I said to Graham. "We've never had a substitute for that long."

"I know," Graham answered. "I wonder who it's going to be."

"Who cares?" David said, moving closer to Graham and me. Then about five other boys leaned in, like they knew David was about to spill a secret or something. "It doesn't matter who it is," David continued. "What matters is all the fun we're going to have for the next week. We can switch names and seats, make up new class rules, and basically do whatever we want. My older brother Gene had a substitute for a week once, and he said it was the best week of his life. The whole class switched seats and names, and the teacher never even knew the difference."

I had heard stories about David's older brother Gene. He made David look like an angel. I heard he was sent to the principal's office so often that he had his own chair there. I heard even David

was scared of him, and David isn't scared of anyone. I wondered if that was why David was such a
bully. Maybe he just picked on me like his brother picked on him. I wasn't so sure I wanted to do
all the crazy things David was talking about, but
I was excited and figured a few harmless pranks
wouldn't hurt.

"Okay, listen up, guys." David spoke in a low
voice as if the substitute were standing nearby.
"Everyone has to choose someone to switch names
with for next week. I'm going to be you," he said,
pointing to Matt Lindenheimer.

"Matt?" I said without thinking. "How can you
be him? He's so smart!" A hush fell over our little
group. Graham elbowed me in the ribs, and every
kid turned to me.

"What's that supposed to mean, dork? Are you
saying I'm not smart enough to pass for Matt?"
David pulled his arm back, ready to slug me.

"No, no," I said, trying to think fast. "That's not
what I meant at all. I was just . . . um . . . thinking that . . . maybe you and I could switch names.
Yeah, that's it—you and I should switch."

David lowered his arm and started laughing. "Right," he said. "I'm sure you'd love to be me for a week, but I don't want some wimpy dork running around with my name." I looked over at Matt Lindenheimer, who seemed at least as wimpy and dorky as me, if not more. He was smiling, like he was proud that David wanted to be him. Just then the bell rang, breaking up our meeting.

We all ran to class thinking of the fun we were going to have next week. After school Graham and I talked about it all the way home.

"This is going to be so great!" Graham said. "A whole week with a substitute. I almost feel sorry for whoever it's going to be."

"Yeah, but I guess that's what being a sub is all about," I said. "They have to know that the kids are going to do crazy things and try to get away with stuff. What do they care anyway? Once they're done, they just get to leave. They aren't really responsible for us learning anything. They're kind of like babysitters. Hey, how about switching names and seats with me?"

"Thanks, but no thanks. I'm going to switch with Brian. His desk is right next to Kelly's. This is my chance to sit by her for a whole week straight," Graham said. "I can't miss out on that."

"Yeah, I guess not. So do you want to hang out and shoot some hoops?"

"Not today," Graham answered. "I'm going to ask my mom if she'll take me to get my hair cut for the school pictures. I'm going to give Kelly one of my pictures, and I want to look my best."

"You're going to give Kelly a picture of you?" I asked.

"Of course. I always do," he said. "Look, I even have one of her in my wallet."

"You have a wallet?" I asked. I'd known Graham forever, and I'd never seen his wallet.

"Sure, where do you think I keep all my money?" Graham answered. He pulled out a thin wallet and opened it up. The place where money should have been was empty. In fact, there was nothing in there at all except an old, scratched-up picture of Kelly.

"Whoa, how old is this?" I said, grabbing the picture. "She looks like a first-grader. She's even missing one of her front teeth."

"Yeah, yeah," Graham said, grabbing the photo and sliding it back into its slot in the empty wallet. "I'm going to ask her for a new one this year. You should get one from Heidi."

We spent the rest of the walk home talking about wallets and pictures. I decided I was going to look my best for this picture too. You know, just in case I got brave enough to ask Heidi for a picture or in case she wanted one from me. That would be cool.

3

One Gatorade, Please

THE NEXT DAY, I woke up excited for baseball. I love the weekday games. I don't know why, I just do. Maybe it's because I would be at home doing homework if I didn't have a game. And today I was ready to play the Tigers. Coach Parker had told me I would be pitching, and I just knew I would get some great hits too. My whole family was coming, even Gramps. I decided that it would be fun to have Heidi and Diane there. For some reason, I felt like everything was going to be great. I got dressed, ate breakfast, gave my mom a hug, and ran down to Graham's house to walk to school. We talked about the game the whole way.

"I think this is the day I hit a home run, *hermano*," I said. "I am feeling lucky today!"

"Me too," Graham said, swinging an invisible bat and watching the invisible ball sail away for a grand slam. "Okay, Raymond," he continued. "When I'm catching today and give you two fingers for my signal, it means throw a fastball. Three fingers means a slider, and this means a curveball." He moved his finger in a circular motion.

"All right," I answered. "But all of my pitches are kind of the same. I think they're fastballs."

"Okay, then what if I always give you the sign for fastball? If I give you something else, like a curveball sign, just shake your head until I give you the right sign," Graham said.

"Yeah, that'll work."

We spent the rest of our walk guessing what the score at our game would be. I thought it would be 8–2 for us. Graham thought it would be more like 12–3. Either way, we knew it would be a great game.

School was slow and boring. I just wanted it to

be over. The only fun part was recess. We all gathered together to go over the plan for next week. This time it was almost our entire class. Even Lizzy was there. The plan was set: we would all change seats and names, we would tell the substitute that every Tuesday and Thursday we get an extra fifteen minutes of recess if we're good, and we would say that we have a class party on Friday that's been planned for months. It was going to be great.

Even better, David was actually talking to me without hitting me or making fun of me. Don't get me wrong—it's not like he was inviting me over to his house after school to hang out. But sometimes during class, he would lean over and talk to me about the plan for next week. Maybe this whole substitute teacher thing would finally help me and David become friends. Or at least make him stop being so mean to me.

After recess, I kept looking at Lizzy, thinking that maybe she was just going along with the plan so she could tell on us—you know, like a spy.

I watched her closely, waiting for her to walk up to Mrs. Gibson's desk and spill the beans on the whole thing just to get a few brownie points. But surprisingly enough, she didn't say a word. This was truly going to be the best week ever.

After school I ran home and got into my baseball uniform. The Giants had blue jerseys with GIANTS written on the front in big white letters and white baseball pants. I was using the same pants from last year, and they still had a big round stain on the back where I'd sat on the wad of gum. We got most of it off, but the circle was still there. There were also a couple of nacho cheese stains on the sides where I'd wiped my hands.

I went to the kitchen to get a glass of milk. There's something about drinking milk that makes me feel stronger. Geri already had the milk carton out.

"Hey, save some of that for me," I said. She filled her glass halfway, paused, then filled it up the rest of the way, using every last drop from the carton.

"Come on, I need that. I've got a game tonight."

"Ooh, is it your magic potion?" Geri laughed. "Does it turn you into Super Dork?"

"Mom!" I screamed.

"I'm right here, sweetie. What do you need?" She walked into the kitchen.

"Geri won't share the milk. And she called me Super Dork."

"Oh, I'm sure she just meant to say that you are super," Mom answered. I could tell she wanted to ignore the fight.

"That's right." Geri smirked. "You're just super, Raymond." Then she walked out of the room.

Graham and I rode our bikes to the field about an hour early to play catch. After a while, the rest of our team started showing up. Once Coach Parker got there, we ran a lap around the field, got into our positions, and warmed up. Coach always ran with us. We'd try to catch him, but he was always too fast for us. We practiced for a while and then let the Tigers use the field.

"Hey, Mom," I called, running out of the dugout. My mom, dad, sister, and grandpa were walking up the sidewalk toward the field. "Can I have some money for a drink?" I pointed to the snack bar that was just opening up.

"Sure, sweetie," she said, reaching into her purse.

"Hold on, partner, I've got you covered," Gramps interrupted, stepping in front of my mom. He dug into his pocket for some money. "Here you go, slugger," he said, pulling out a whole handful of stuff. He opened his big, wrinkly hand and sorted through rubber bands, string, crumpled paper, keys, and pocket fuzz to find the money.

"Whoa, Gramps, what *don't* you keep in your pocket?" Dad said. "You don't have Grandma in that pile somewhere, do you?"

Gramps was too busy going through the handful of stuff to answer. Somehow he was able to find about two dollars in coins. I put my hands together, and Gramps dropped the money into them. I also got some of the pocket fuzz.

"Thanks, Gramps." I ran over to the snack bar and was the first in line.

Luke's mom was working at the snack bar. Luke is in our class at school, and he's on the Giants. His mom was always a little grumpy. One time last season, I bought some nachos and she would only give me one napkin. I tried to take more, but she grabbed them right out of my hand and stuffed them back into the metal napkin holder.

"Just one napkin, please. They cost money, you know," she said.

"I thought they were free," I answered, trying to reach for another. She grabbed the napkin holder and took it away before I could get more.

"They may be free to you, but someone has to pay for them," she said, not giving in. I stood there for a minute or two waiting for her to put the napkins back, but she never did. Finally I just walked away. Have you ever tried to eat nachos with only one napkin? It's impossible. You need at least three: one for each hand and one for your face. And that's only if you are really careful. That's where the nacho cheese stains on the sides of my pants came from.

So today I was playing it safe. "One Gatorade, please," I said.

"What flavor?" Luke's mom answered. She rolled her eyes and recited all six flavors in about two seconds.

"How about the bright yellow?" I said happily. I love yellow Gatorade.

"Bright yellow isn't a flavor, it's a color," she said with a sour look. But obviously she knew what I was talking about, because she set the bright yellow Gatorade down right in front of me. "That's a dollar fifty," she said. I dumped the pile of coins and fuzz onto the counter, separated the dollar fifty, and slid it toward her. As she counted my money I looked around to see if Heidi and Diane had shown up yet, but there was no sign of them. I grabbed my Gatorade and gathered up the extra coins. I left a big piece of fuzz on the counter. "There's your tip." I laughed quietly to myself as I walked away. I thought it was pretty funny.

It was time to start the game. I ran back to the dugout, grabbed my glove, and hurried out to the pitcher's mound. After about ten practice pitches, I was ready and the game began. Graham was playing catcher as usual.

"*Play ball!*" the umpire called out. The batter stepped up to the plate, and Graham immediately started in on him.

"Come on, Raymond," Graham yelled. "This guy stinks. He can't hit." Then he gave me the sign for a fastball.

I wound up and threw the ball as fast as I could.

"Strike one!" the ump yelled. The batter didn't even swing.

"He's scared of you, Raymond. Give him another strike, he's too scared to swing," Graham yelled again, laughing.

The second ball was high and outside, but the batter swung.

"Strike two! The count is 0 and 2," the ump said, holding up a fist on one hand and two fingers on the other.

"Sorry, batter," Graham said. "Does it bother

you when I talk? I won't say a word this time, and we'll see if you can hit. Okay, everyone be really quiet so number eight can concentrate on the ball." The batter looked completely frustrated. Graham really knew how to make the batters crazy.

The batter swung as hard as he could at the last pitch.

"Strike three, batter's out," the ump shouted. Our fans cheered. Carlos's dad yelled something in Spanish. I assumed he was cheering. Grandpa followed by screaming *"Muy bien!"* and then high-fived Carlos's dad.

"Time-out," Graham said to the ump. He got up and headed toward the pitcher's mound.

"Graham, what are you doing? I'm throwing great," I said.

"I just wanted to ask if you've seen the girls." He glanced over toward our fans on the small, wooden bleachers. "Kelly said she would be here."

"I haven't seen them. But who cares? We're having a great game," I said.

"I know, I just thought I would ask, since you can probably see better from up here on the pitcher's mound," Graham said. "Plus, it makes the batter think we're doing something sneaky when I come out here."

"Let's go," yelled the ump.

"Okay, okay," Graham said, smiling. "Smile like we have something up our sleeves," he whispered to me before he walked back to the plate.

I tried to smile, but it was hard. For some reason, if I try to smile when I don't feel like smiling, it always comes out weird. Graham got down behind the plate and gave me a sign for a curveball or something. I shook my head and waited for the fastball sign. Then something broke my concentration.

"Are you all right, Raymond?" I heard my mom yell, standing up in the bleachers. "You look like you don't feel well!" My dad pulled her down to her seat.

Oh man, I thought. *I knew my fake smile looked weird.* I stopped smiling and gave a little thumbs-up to my mom. She smiled, and everything was back to normal.

My first two pitches to the next batter were

really bad, but he swung at both of them. His coach yelled at him to swing at only the good ones. Finally, I got one over the plate, and the batter watched it fly by without swinging.

"Strike three!" the ump called, sending the kid to his dugout.

The next guy hit a hard line drive right to our shortstop, who caught the ball for the last out.

"Yes!" I hissed under my breath. "Three up, three down. No problem." Things were looking good.

Coach Gramps

"**THAT WAS GREAT** work in the field, boys. Now we need some hits!" Coach Parker told us. Then he walked out of the dugout and stood in front of the bleachers. "Could I get a volunteer to help coach first base?" he asked the crowd. Zach's dad usually helps coach, but with Zach out, he wasn't there. All the parents looked around at each other, but no one raised a hand.

"I'll do it!" came a scratchy voice from the back of the stands. It sounded like Gramps. I stood up and looked back. Not only did it sound like Gramps, it *was* Gramps.

"Nice, your grandpa's going to help. I love that old dude," Graham said.

"Yeah, me too," I agreed. "It's just that you never know what he's going to say or do."

"I know." Graham grinned. "That's why I like him."

Gramps looked excited to help. He had told me a zillion stories about when he played baseball back in the olden days.

"Hi, Gramps," I said as he came around the fence.

"That's 'Coach' to you, sonny," he said, passing me. He grabbed a hat from the bench and adjusted it to fit his bald head.

"Hey, that's my hat," Kevin complained. He had just set his hat down to put on a batting helmet. Gramps didn't answer and walked straight out to coach first base.

The umpire got back into position behind the catcher.

"Batter up."

Kevin walked up to the plate, took a few practice swings, and waited for the throw. He swung and hit the first pitch. The third baseman threw the ball. It was close.

"Out!" came the official call.

"What do you mean, out?" Gramps argued. "He was safe! What's wrong with you? Did you even see the play?"

"Sir, the runner was out. Play ball!"

Gramps said some things under his breath and returned to his spot by first base.

I was up next and strolled to the plate confidently. I knew I could hit off this pitcher. I let the first pitch go by.

"Strike one," the ump called out.

"Are you blind? That was in the dirt!" Gramps began again. "How much is this other team paying you to make calls like that?"

"Time-out," the umpire announced, raising his hands in the air. He walked up to Gramps and removed his mask. "Listen, sir," he said, "please let me call the game, and let the kids have fun."

"How can they have fun if you're giving the game away to the other team?" Gramps shouted. By then Coach Parker had run up and pushed his big body between Gramps and the ump. I couldn't tell what he said, but they all calmed down and went back to their spots. Now Gramps started hounding the pitcher. He said things like, "This guy can't throw!" and "Who taught you to pitch, your grandma?" It must have worked, because the next four pitches were all balls.

I walked to first base.

"Okay, I want you to steal second on this pitch," Gramps said. "Just listen for my signal. I'll tell you when to run."

I took a couple of steps off first base and waited for Gramps's signal. As the pitcher started his windup, I heard the loudest, most terrifying noise I have ever heard in my life. It was Gramps.

"RUUUNNNN!!!" he screeched. His voice was cracking, and he sounded like he was being attacked by killer bees. It was so scary that I fell to the ground trying to get away. He kept screaming. "RUN! NOW! RUN!" I finally made it back to my feet and started running. The catcher threw the ball. I knew it would be close, so I slid.

"OUT!" screamed the ump.

"What? He was safe!" Gramps screamed back.

The ump threw off his mask and ran up to Gramps. They both yelled at each other, and then the ump pointed to the bleachers. I couldn't believe it. He had just kicked my grandpa out of the game. Gramps headed off the field. As he passed the bench he took off his hat and stuck it back on Kevin's head. Then he found his spot back on the bleachers.

"Oooh, gross, old man sweat," Kevin said. He took off the hat and wiped his head with his arm.

Gramps sat back down next to my mom and dad. He was smiling and talking to the other parents. It was like nothing had even happened. Graham came and sat by me on the bench.

"See," he said. "That was great! Your grandpa is the best!"

I opened my Gatorade and took a swig. Just then Graham grabbed my shoulder to pull himself up, making me spill my Gatorade all over the front of my pants.

"She's here!" Graham said. "Kelly's here! And

Heidi and Diane are walking up the sidewalk. This game is just getting better!"

I could feel the cold Gatorade in my lap. "Hey, you made me spill my Gatorade all over my pants! And it's bright yellow!"

"Oh, sorry, Raymond," Graham said. "It was an accident—whoa, look at your pants."

"I know, I know. Everyone's going to think I . . . you know," I said.

"No, they won't. No one will even notice. You'll be fine," Graham said. Heidi, Diane, and Kelly walked up to the fence.

Graham tipped his hat to the girls like they do in cowboy movies. "Enjoying the game?" I turned my back to them so they wouldn't see my pants.

"Hi, Raymond," Heidi said.

"Oh, hey, Heidi," I answered, hoping she wouldn't think I was weird for not turning toward them.

"Hey, Raymond, don't be weird. Come over here," Graham said. He grabbed my shoulders and turned me around. Diane started laughing.

"Back on the field, everyone," Coach interrupted. "Same positions as last inning. Raymond, get on the mound." He tossed me a ball.

I turned and walked out of the dugout and toward the pitcher's mound. Graham hurried up to the plate, and we started warming up. I didn't hear any laughing from the other team, so I figured they couldn't see the bright yellow wet spot on the front of my pants. Then, from the corner of my eye, I saw someone waving from the bleachers. I looked up and saw my mom trying to get my attention. I gave her a little wave and went back to warming up. After another throw I heard a *"Psst!"* from the same place. I looked over and could tell my mom was trying to say something.

"What?" I whispered to her. I couldn't tell what she was trying to say. Now she was mouthing it even bigger, with her mouth stretched open as far as it could go.

I looked away and tried to ignore her. I figured I could talk to her between innings.

"She's saying *bathroom*! She wants to know if

you need to go to the *bathroom!*" Gramps yelled. "Look at your pants!"

Everyone in the whole place started laughing.

"IT'S GATORADE!" I yelled. "I SPILLED GATO-RADE!"

"Yeah, sure it is," I heard someone say from the Tigers' dugout. Then they all cracked up even louder.

"All right, batter up," the ump yelled, wiping tears of laughter from his eyes. It seemed that my little wet pants episode was all the Tigers needed to get their confidence back. The first six batters hit the ball, and in no time it was 4–0 in their favor. Coach pulled me from the mound and put in Kevin. They got one more hit, and then we were able to get the next three batters out.

The game got worse from there. It was the bottom of the last inning, and we were down by five runs. There were two outs, and I was up to bat. The bases were loaded. A home run would bring us within one run. I was feeling gross. My pants were yellow, people were still laughing at me, and worst of all, the girl I really liked was sitting in the stands watching this whole disaster. I took a deep breath and stepped up to the plate. If there was ever a time I needed a hit, it was now. I dug in my back foot and pulled the bat back.

The first pitch was perfect. I could tell as soon as it left the pitcher's hand. I whipped the bat around as fast as I could and . . . POW! I smacked the ball. It went soaring through the air toward right field. I started jogging to first base, knowing that this would be my first grand slam ever. Then some words that ruined the moment rang through the air.

"Foul ball!"

There were a lot of *ooohs* coming from our bleachers and dugout.

"Nice hit, Raymond," Coach said, patting me on the helmet as I passed by on my way back to the plate. "Straighten it out this time."

I picked up the bat and took my place at the plate again. The next pitch was really high. I started to swing but caught myself.

"Ball!"

The next pitch came in perfect. I swung so

hard I almost fell over. Unfortunately, I missed the ball.

"Strike two!" the ump called.

I was getting nervous. One more strike and I'd be out.

The next ball looked perfect too, but I didn't swing.

"Outside. Ball. Two balls, two strikes." The ump held up two fingers on both hands. The Tigers' coach complained that it should have been a strike. Then he asked for a time-out and walked up to talk to the pitcher. Coach Parker came over to talk to me too.

"Hey, bud. Be a swinger in there. If it's close, give it a ride. You know you can do it." There was something about Coach Parker that made me think he was always right about baseball stuff. So I stood there confidently waiting for the next pitch as both coaches went back to their spots.

The next pitch was almost in the ground. I let it go for ball three. One more pitch. I was really nervous. I could hear our fans cheering me on—

Mom, Dad, Diane, Heidi, and Kelly. Gramps had a mouthful of nachos and was screaming something I couldn't understand. Whatever it was, I'm sure it was good.

"Last pitch. If it's close, you've got to be swinging, bud," Coach yelled out. As the pitcher threw the last ball, it looked a little high, but something inside told me to swing. I swung as hard as I could. This time I hit the ball. It flew straight toward center field. There was no way this was going to be a foul ball.

I threw the bat down and raced past first base and toward second. The center fielder yelled, "got it," as the ball sailed toward him. I rounded first base figuring I was going to be out. Luckily, the ball hit his mitt and fell to the ground. As I got to second base I heard Coach Parker yelling to keep going.

"Slide, slide!" Coach screamed as I got close to third base. Just as I slid, I saw the ball land in the dirt and bounce past the third baseman. As he ran to get the ball I jumped up and ran toward home.

I was halfway there when the ball was thrown home. The catcher caught it and stood there waiting to tag me. I quickly turned back and ran toward third base. I could tell this was not going to end well.

Just then I saw the ball fly over my head and land in the third baseman's mitt. I was caught between third and home. Before the third baseman could tag me, I stopped and turned for home again. This time I wasn't going to stop. I slid just as I heard the ball hit the catcher's mitt. I lay there in the dirt and stared at the ump. The catcher held his glove with the ball on my leg. Finally the dust cleared and the ump made his call: "Safe!"

Yes! I jumped up. A grand slam! Right there in front of my team, my family, the girls, Luke's grumpy mom at the snack bar—everyone. My teammates ran out of the dugout, and we all jumped around together for a few seconds. I could see Heidi and Diane standing up clapping. It was the greatest moment of my life. Even with a big yellow spot on the front of my pants.

"Your turn, *hermano*!" I said to Graham, who was walking up to the plate.

"Thanks," he said. Then, turning to Kelly in the front row of the bleachers, he said, "This one's for you," and gave her a wink. I just laughed and ran to the dugout and slid down the bench.

"Nice hit, Raymond," Heidi said from the stands.

"Thanks, I—"

"That's the way to swing that bat," Gramps interrupted, swinging an invisible bat. He almost swung himself right off the bleachers. Dad grabbed him by the arm.

"Yep, just like your old grandpa back in the day," Dad added.

"Thanks, Gramps!"

I turned back to the game to cheer Graham on.

Graham had a huge smile on his face. His run would tie it all up. He needed to get on base and make it all the way around to keep us in the game. The first three pitches were balls. I could tell he didn't want to walk. He wanted a home run.

"Come on, give me something to hit!" he yelled at the pitcher. Our whole team was on its feet. The next pitch was high, but Graham swung anyway.

"Strike one!" the ump called out.

"Come on, give me a good one!" Graham called out again, pounding the plate with his bat. The pitcher took a deep breath and threw as hard as he could. Graham swung hard. It was a line drive to the second baseman, who caught the ball without even having to move. Graham just stood there at home plate. He didn't even have time to run. The game was over, and he was the last one out. I walked up to him and told him "good try." It didn't seem to cheer him up. He just stood there looking out toward the outfield where his ball was supposed to go.

"Come on, Graham, let's go," I said. I put my arm around his shoulders, and we walked back to the dugout. We grabbed our bats and gloves. Our parents gave us the ol' "good game" and "you'll get 'em next time" routine. Kelly left to go finish watching her little brother's baseball game at the other end of the park. Diane and Heidi normally would've teased Graham, but they could tell he wasn't up to it.

"At least you didn't have to buy me a candy bar," Diane said. She slapped Graham on the back.

"Yeah, that was just a lucky catch," Heidi said as they headed off. "See you guys at school."

"Nice game, but you might want to work on your bladder control," cackled Geri. I could tell it would take her a long time to forget about my wet-pants episode.

"I told you that umpire was rooting for the other team," Gramps said.

"Oh, come on, Dad, they're just kids. They're here to have fun," said Mom. "Right, sweetie?" she added, taking my bat and glove from my arms. "I'll take these home with me."

"Thanks, Mom," I said. Graham and I grabbed our bikes and started down the road. It was a silent ride home. Now we had lost two games. Our final year in the minors just couldn't end this way.

5

Say Cheese

THE REST OF the week was pretty boring. Then Friday came and it was picture day. I wanted a good picture this year. Last year my mom, who is not a professional haircutter, decided she would cut my hair the night before pictures. Let's just say that didn't go so well. My hair was long in some places, almost shaved off in others, and on top there were a few places where the hair stood straight up. I looked like a weirdo. The worst part is that my picture is hanging proudly in our family room for everyone to see. It's also on my grandparents' wall. I couldn't wait to get a new picture this year. Plus, I had been thinking about what

Graham had said. You know, about asking Heidi for a picture and giving her one of mine. I decided that's what I would do.

This year's pictures were going to be perfect. The day before, my mom took me to a real place to get my hair cut. After that, she took me to the clothing store, and we bought a brand-new shirt. She let me pick it out and everything. It was a golf shirt. They didn't have the dark blue one I wanted in my size, but the store lady found a light blue one in the back room.

On Friday, I walked to Graham's house before school as usual. I had to wait about five minutes for him to finish getting ready. When he finally came out, I almost didn't recognize him.

"Whoa, what happened to you?" I asked, trying not to laugh. His hair looked all wet and wavy.

"What do you think?" he said with a huge smile on his face. Obviously, he didn't think he looked as crazy as I thought he did.

"Um . . . well . . . it's different," I said. "You know, just really . . . different."

"Yeah, it's awesome!" Graham said. "I wanted to look really good for my picture, so I was looking at this magazine at the haircutting place and I saw a cool guy with hair like this and I told the lady that's what I wanted. My mom tried to talk me out of it, but she finally gave in."

"So what did they do? How did it get all wavy?" I asked. "And why is your hair so stiff?" I added, touching the hard red waves on his head.

"It's gel," Graham said proudly. "All the movie stars and people like that use it. It's supposed to keep my hair looking like this all day. I have a whole bottle of it. Do you want some for your hair?"

"No way!" I said. "I mean . . . no, thank you. You should save it all for yours." We started walking quickly to school.

"By the way, check out this new shirt I got last night," I said.

"Yeah, I noticed it when I first saw you," Graham said. "It looks a little . . . um . . ."

"A little what?" I asked.

"You know . . . the color," Graham said. "That light blue looks kind of . . ."

"Kind of cool?" I said, finishing his sentence for him. "Yeah, I thought so too. At first I wanted dark blue, but they didn't have any more in my size. But luckily the store lady told us to wait for a minute and she left and came back with this one."

Graham had a weird look on his face, like he wanted to say something but just couldn't get it out. By then, though, it was almost time for the bell to ring, so we ran the last block and made it to school just in time. We both walked through the classroom door at the exact same second. Some-one immediately yelled out "nice hair," and the sound of giggling started filling the room.

"Thank you very much," Graham replied, giv-ing a big thumbs-up sign to the class without realizing they were probably laughing at him. He walked happily to his desk, giving a little wink to Kelly as he passed by. I walked to my desk and sat down.

David's desk was back by mine again. "That's a

pretty shirt, Raymond," David said, trying to talk in a girl's voice. "You know I would punch you, but I don't hit girls."

"What are you talking about?" I said. I looked around the room. Everyone was either staring at Graham and his new wavy hairdo or looking at me. There was only one person who wasn't laughing: Lizzy. She just had a mad look on her face and was glaring at me.

I looked at her, wondering what her problem was. Then I noticed her shirt. It was light blue and looked kind of familiar. *Oh my gosh!* I suddenly screamed in my brain. *I'm wearing the same shirt as LIZZY! I'M WEARING A GIRL'S SHIRT!* I couldn't believe it. How could they sell me a girl's shirt? That just seems wrong. I'll bet that's where that store lady went to find the shirt—the girls' department!

This is just great! I thought. *Last year I had a lousy haircut, and this year I'm dressed like a girl!* Why didn't my mom tell me it was a girl's shirt? Surely she must have known. I mean, she's a girl. Anyway, it was too late to change shirts. Mrs. Gibson had just started lining us up to walk down to the lunchroom where they would take our pictures.

I looked closer at Lizzy. She was wearing a white skirt and a hair bow that matched her shirt—I mean, my shirt. The whole outfit actually looked good on Lizzy. I looked down at my own outfit, and it seemed to look stranger and stranger the longer I looked.

I walked back by Graham. "Man, did you see what Lizzy is wearing?" I asked. "Did you think I was wearing a girl's shirt when you saw me this morning?"

"Well, kind of," Graham said. "But you looked so happy that I didn't want to make you feel bad. If I knew Lizzy would be wearing the same shirt, I would've definitely told you. But how could I know you and Lizzy would have the same fashion taste?"

We walked down the hall in single file to the multipurpose room. It was the usual school picture scene: most of the lights off; some big, silver, umbrella-like things on one side of the room; and the risers with the big blue backdrop. Mrs. Gibson lined us up by height. The tallest were directed to the top of the risers. I was in that group, along with David, Diane, Lizzy, and Zach. The medium-size kids were on the next level, and the shortest were in the front. That was Graham, Suzy, Brad, and a couple of other shorties.

The photographer stood back for a better look. "Okay, let's move this young lady in the front over here." He was talking about Suzy. She quickly moved over by Graham.

He stood back again and squinted. "Hmm, let's see. Back row, let's scoot in a little closer. And would you in the blue shirt switch places with the young man on the end?"

I stepped forward and tried to squeeze past Diane to get to the end.

"Wait," the photographer interrupted. "Not you. I meant this young lady in the blue shirt." I was even confusing myself with Lizzy in this shirt.

Finally we were all in the right spots, and the photographer took about five pictures. Then we lined up for the individual photos. David was first. He stood there with a scowl on his face. The photographer tried to make him laugh and told him to say cheese and pizza and a bunch of other things, but his face never budged. Finally, the guy gave up and just took the picture with David's grumpy look.

I stood by Graham and Heidi waiting for our turns. Graham asked me if his hair was still okay or if it had gotten messed up. Heidi and I looked at it and then looked at each other. We both smiled, and I could tell she was thinking the same thing I was.

"Well, I'm not exactly sure how it's supposed to look. But it's still all wavy and stiff," I said. I touched the top of his hair. It was hard as a rock.

"Perfect," Graham said. "These pictures are going to be great."

"Yeah," I said. "Except for the fact that Lizzy and I are twins today."

"No, you're not," Heidi said. "You're not twins at all."

"Thanks," I answered. That made me feel a little better.

"'Cause she's wearing a matching bow," Heidi said, chuckling. "I'm just kidding, your shirt looks fine. Hey, Diane, Raymond's shirt doesn't look like a girl's shirt, does it?"

Diane walked over. "No, it absolutely looks like a boy's shirt," she said. "But do you think I can borrow it tomorrow?" She and Heidi both busted up. Then Graham followed. I stood there feeling sorry for myself for a moment, but then something came over me and I started laughing. If Heidi and Diane could laugh at my shirt, why couldn't I? It actually cheered me up.

Just then Lizzy walked by. "What's so funny?" she said in her snooty voice.

"Nothing, except that I'm wearing your shirt," I said between laughs. Lizzy flipped her curls and stormed away.

By the time it was my turn to get my picture taken, I was still smiling from my girl shirt and didn't even have to say cheese.

The Substitute

WE HAD ANOTHER baseball game on Saturday. My mom washed my baseball pants twice trying to get all the stains out. Fortunately, all of the Gatorade came off, but the gum spot and nacho cheese stains were still there. The game was great—we killed the Cubs. I pitched most of the game and got two hits, and Graham even hit a home run. Finally, a win. But we would need a lot more wins if there was going to be any chance of saving this season. Not only did my family behave this time, but after the game my dad took me and Graham to get ice cream. It was a perfect day.

On the way home, Graham and I sat in the

backseat talking about how much fun we were going to have with the substitute the next week. We talked quietly so my dad wouldn't hear us.

"Hey, what are you two whispering about back there? Must be talking about girls," Dad said, smiling at us in the rearview mirror.

"Nope. Just secret stuff," Graham said. "We can't tell you or we'd have to kill you."

This week was going to be hilarious. I wondered if we could all really get away with trading places with each other for an entire week. And if we'd really be able to have a party on Friday. I was feeling sorry for the substitute already. But I figured that since we weren't going to do anything mean, it would be okay.

"So are you still trading places with Brian?" I asked Graham when we were back at my house, hanging out in my room.

"Nope. At first I traded with him so I could sit next to Kelly," Graham said. "But then I found out that Kelly was trading with Diane. So I switched again with Brad, who sits next to Diane. It was kind of confusing, but I think it's going to work out."

"Well, I traded with Luke," I said, "so you can just call me Luke the Puke for the next week." Luke moved to our school in the fall, and when he introduced himself to the class, he turned kind of greenish and threw up all over the floor. So unfortunately for him, he got stuck with the nickname Luke the Puke.

Monday couldn't come soon enough. I was so excited I couldn't even sleep the night before. And on top of it all, on Sunday night Mom said she had a fun surprise for me. She wouldn't tell me what it was yet. When Monday morning finally came, I jumped out of bed, ate breakfast, brushed my teeth, and ran out the door. "Bye, Mom," I said as I slammed the door.

"Bye, sweetie," I heard her call back from the kitchen. I ran all the way to Graham's house. He was already out in his driveway waiting for me.

"This is it, *hermano*," I said. "Are you ready?"

"You know it," Graham said, nodding his head.

His red, curly hair was bouncing all over the place. Luckily, he had finally run out of gel. "This week will go down in history as the greatest week ever at East Millcreek Elementary School."

We spent the whole walk to school talking like the people we were trading desks with. Graham tried to make his hair stand up and talked in his best Brad Shaw voice. I introduced myself as Luke and pretended to throw up all over Graham. I thought our acting was really good.

We finally made it to school and walked into our classroom. Everyone was at different desks around the room. Like us, they were all excited about our prank. People were laughing and joking around with each other. The only problem was that school was about to start and there was still no substitute. There was no Mrs. Gibson either. When the bell finally rang, everyone sat down and just looked at each other. Then the principal, Mr. Worley, walked in.

"Hello, boys and girls," he said in his big, loud voice. "I know Mrs. Gibson told you she would be away for the next week." We all looked at Mr. Worley, afraid that *he* was going to be our substitute for the week. That would be terrible. It would be nonstop stories of his army days. I thought we might literally die of boredom from an entire week of Mr. Worley's stories. By the looks on everyone's faces, I could tell that we were all thinking the same thing.

"Well, kids," he said, placing his large, plump hand on top of David's head (David was now in the front row). "Your substitute will be here shortly. Why don't you all take out your reading books and read silently while you wait for her." Everyone was quiet except for Graham. He was leaning over and talking to Kelly.

"That means you, young man," Mr. Worley said, bringing his hand down on Graham's new desk hard and loud. Graham jumped.

"Yes, sir!" Graham yelled out, looking startled.

"At ease, soldier," Mr. Worley replied, smiling. Then he gave one last glance around the room and walked out the door. You could hear everyone exhale a loud sigh of relief. We all looked into our new desks to find reading books. I pulled out Luke's book, hoping it would be interesting. Unfortunately, it was *Charlotte's Web.* The librarian had told me once that I should read that book, but somehow the picture on the front never looked too exciting to me. It was just a girl, a pig, and a spider. Just as I was about to break open the book, Matt Lindenheimer, who was sitting by the door, yelled, "She's coming!"

We had talked about this moment every day at recess for the past week, and we were ready. We all tried to act serious, but we couldn't hold back our smiles. There was a lot of giggling and wiggling around in seats. The sound of a lady's footsteps got closer and closer. Then, when I could hardly stand it anymore, our substitute came bursting through the doorway.

"Hello, class!" she called out in a bright, happy voice. I looked up and felt all the blood drain from my face. I thought I was going to faint. There was only one thing to say.

"*Mom?*" I said. My mom, my very own mom, was our substitute! My hopes and dreams of being Luke the Puke for the week were dashed. I couldn't believe it. She had sent me to school this morning without saying a word about this! Surely she knew ahead of time. Surely she didn't just decide to ruin the best week of my life sometime between the moment I left our house this morning and right now.

"Mrs. Knudson?" Graham said. "What are you doing here? Did you see our substitute out there in the hall?"

"I *am* the substitute, Graham," Mom answered with a big smile. Then she looked at me. "Raymond, this is the surprise I was telling you about yesterday. Surprise! Isn't this great?" The entire class was staring at me. I could tell by the angry looks on their faces that they blamed me for spoiling their week of fun.

"How is everyone today?" Mom asked, walking over to Mrs. Gibson's desk. "Well, hello, Diane, Heidi, and oh, Lizzy, how is your mother doing?"

Diane gave her a sad wave, and Heidi said hello. I don't know what happened to Lizzy, but all of a sudden it was like my mom turned into Mrs. Gibson and Lizzy was trying to become the teacher's pet again.

"Hi, Mrs. Knudson," Lizzy said. "Thank you for being our substitute. I bet you'll be great."

"Why, thank you, Lizzy," Mom said. "That's very nice of you."

David looked at me from across the room. He was gritting his teeth and hitting his fist into his other hand. My arm started hurting just thinking about what was in store for me at recess. This was going to be a long week.

Sorry, Sweetie

EVERYONE WAS QUIET at morning recess. It was like they had all just found out that Christmas had been canceled. Kids who normally played tag or swung on swings were just moping around. Graham and I usually played basketball at recess, but we didn't really feel up to it today.

"I can't believe your mom is our substitute," Graham said, shaking his head. "You know she ruined all our fun, don't you?"

"Of course I know she ruined our fun!" I said. "This was supposed to be the best week ever, and now everyone is just mad." Just then David walked up and slugged me on the arm.

"That's for wrecking our awesome week. And this," he added, punching me again in the same place, "is just for being a dork."

"David!" called a sharp voice from the school steps. "That was not a nice thing to do to Raymond! I know your mother very well, and I don't think she would appreciate a phone call from me about her son punching other children at recess!" It was my mom, and she was mad. We all turned around and watched as she marched right up to us.

"Now what seems to be the problem, young man?" she asked David. He didn't answer. I knew this was going to end up with more punches to my arm sometime when my mom wasn't around. She just stood there waiting for an answer. Finally David spoke up.

"There's no problem," he grumbled.

"Well, then I think you owe someone an apology," Mom said with her hands on her hips. We were all silent. I could tell David wasn't sure what to do. Usually, Mrs. Gibson just makes him sit by her desk for a day or two.

"Yes, ma'am," David answered. He looked mad. "Sorry, Raymond," he said. Then he turned and walked away.

"Whoa!" Graham burst out laughing. "That was awesome! I've never heard David apologize to anyone. Did you see his face?" Graham made a mad face to imitate David.

"It's not funny and it's not awesome, Graham," Mom said. "Punching other kids is serious business."

"Yeah, but you're not really going to call his mom, are you?" I begged her.

"No, not this time. Hopefully, he's learned his lesson."

After recess, we all came in and sat in our regular places. It wasn't fun switching places when my mom knew who most of us were anyway. David sat down next to me and whispered "You're going to get it!" in my ear. Mom looked at me, but I just gave her a smile to let her know everything was all right.

Graham was a little mad because he still

wanted to sit by Kelly. Kelly, on the other hand, looked kind of happy to have Graham back in his normal spot. Just as Mom started writing our spelling words on the board, David raised his hand.

"By the way," he said. "Did Mrs. Gibson tell you about the party she promised us this Friday? We've been planning it for months." Mom walked back to Mrs. Gibson's desk and picked up the folder of instructions for the next week.

"I don't see anything in here that mentions a party," Mom said, looking at the calendar.

"Well, she did promise us," he said. "You can ask anyone."

"Okay," Mom said, looking around.

Don't ask me, don't ask me, don't ask me, I repeated in my head.

"Raymond," Mom finally called out. My heart sank. "Is this true about a party?" Every eye in the class was on me. I could tell they were begging me to confirm David's story. But how could I lie to my mom? I mean, she always knows when I'm lying. If she caught me, I'd be in trouble for lying *and* we still wouldn't get the party. But if I did lie and for some reason I didn't get caught, everyone would love me. I would be the hero of the day. *Oh man*, I thought to myself, *this stinks!* As badly as I wanted to be the hero, I just couldn't do it. After all, Mom was so excited to be my substitute. How could I let her down? So what if everyone would be mad at me? I decided to do the right thing and tell the truth. And I felt good about it too.

I proudly looked up at my mom, ready to tell her that we were not planning a party. But just as I was about to spoil our fun, Lizzy beat me to it.

"Mrs. Knudson," Lizzy blurted out, holding her hand up. She never waits to be called on—she just raises her hand and starts talking. "I think you should know that we are *not* supposed to have a party. It's just something that the students were trying to trick you into doing." There was a soft groan from the rest of the class, and everyone just hung their heads.

I couldn't believe it! In my heart I actually wanted to do the right thing, even if it meant a slug in the arm and having everyone else in the class be mad at me, and Lizzy had ruined it. Mom looked at me with a disappointed expression on her face. Then she turned to Lizzy.

"Thank you, Lizzy," Mom said. "I appreciate your help."

"No problem," Lizzy answered. "You can tell Mrs. Gibson that I helped you if you want."

I looked around the room. People were still looking at me like they were mad. It was like they were madder at me for not telling my mom that we were supposed to have a party than they were at Lizzy for telling the truth. I didn't get it.

With the party thing out of the way, we all got back to work. Mom gave us the math assignment and told us we had until lunchtime to work on it. About five minutes later, my mom asked for a volunteer to bring some papers to the office. My hand shot up in an instant. This part of having my mom as the teacher would come in handy, I figured. I would get to do all the fun stuff.

"Brad," Mom said, passing right over me. "Can you please take these papers to Ms. Adams in the office? She'll know what they are."

I couldn't believe it. I sat there frozen, my hand

still in the air. What was that about? Was I getting punished for not telling the truth quickly enough earlier? Did my mom forget I was her son?

"Raymond," Mom finally called out. "May I see you for a moment?"

"Oooh, busted," David said as I stood up. Slowly, I dragged my feet to her desk. I couldn't believe it was still only the first day of Mom being my substitute. It already seemed like forever.

"Hi, sweetie," Mom started. I heard a few kids giggle and repeat "sweetie" under their breath. Mom noticed too. "Let's talk out in the hall," she said.

"I will be right back," she told the class. "Please keep working on your fractions and decimals." I followed Mom out into the hall and down by the front doors of the school.

"I'm sorry, sweetie," Mom said with a sad look on her face. "I know you're disappointed that I didn't call on you to run my errand to the office, but just because you're my son, it wouldn't be fair for me to call on you for all the fun things. Do you understand?" she asked.

"Not really," I answered. "I mean, who cares

about fair? You're my mom. I should get some privileges for you being our teacher."

"Well, I'm sorry, sweetie," she said, putting her arm around my shoulder. "I'll try to find something fun for you to do sometime this week." Then she gave me a kiss on the top of my head.

"Whoa, not in school, Mom! Someone might see you! Remember my baseball game last summer?" But it was too late. Brad Shaw had been walking back from the office and saw the whole thing. I turned just in time to see him snickering as he went back into the classroom. "Great," I said under my breath.

"Of course I remember your baseball game last year. And I still don't understand it," she said. "Since when has it been a crime for a mother to give her son a kiss for good luck? Are you embarrassed that your mother loves you?"

"It's not that," I said. "It's just that, you know, it's not cool when you're my age to have your mom give you a kiss in public."

"Well, if people don't think you're cool because

I gave you a kiss, then you don't need to be cool as far as I'm concerned."

What's that supposed to mean? I thought to myself. I *did* want to be cool. And I sure didn't want to give up being cool just so I could get a kiss on the top of my head.

"But, Mom," I said. "It's just that people make fun—"

"Oh, don't worry about what people say, sweetie," she said, cutting me off.

"And by the way," I said, "when you call me 'sweetie' in class, I was wondering if maybe . . . you know . . ."

"Say no more, sweetie—I mean, Raymond. For the next week, I promise I will not embarrass you anymore." I didn't believe her, since embarrassing me seemed to be part of her nature, but I hoped for the best.

"Thanks, Mom," I said. Then we both returned to class. She kept her word and didn't embarrass me for the rest of the day. Unfortunately, there were still four more days left.

A Stinky Lunch

THE NEXT DAY started out well. Mom passed back our exercises on fractions and decimals. I got 100 percent on mine. Then she asked David to come to her desk while we all worked on the new math assignment. It looked like Mom was going over his assignment with him. During our government unit in social studies, she let us all write letters to the governor. She even brought a roll of stamps for us to stick on the letters. Then it was time for lunch.

Graham and I had our usual competition of guessing what was for lunch as we walked down the hall. "Smells like burritos," I said.

"Are you crazy? It's definitely chicken nuggets," Graham said with confidence. We walked into the lunchroom and immediately saw chicken nuggets on the trays.

"Told you," Graham said. Since I bring my lunch, I ran over and found a spot for us at our regular table and saved room for Graham and some of our friends. Zach sat down across from me.

"Hey, I heard you pitched a great game on Saturday," he said.

"Yeah, it was awesome! Graham even hit a home run!" I said. "At this rate, I think we could win the championship."

"I know we can. I just hope my finger gets better by then," Zach said, examining his finger all wrapped up. "Plus, these bandages are really starting to smell."

"Let me smell," I said. My nose met his broken finger halfway across the table, and I took a big whiff. "Ugh, that's terrible!" I gagged.

Just then Graham set his tray down next to me. "What's going on?" he asked.

"Smell those rotten bandages on Zach's finger," I said. "They're disgusting!"

Graham looked at me like I was crazy. "Why would I want to smell them after you just told me they're disgusting?"

"I don't know," I said. "Probably for the same reason I wanted to smell his finger after Zach told me it stinks."

We sat there for about a minute until Graham couldn't take it any longer. "All right, all right, let me smell that finger," he burst out. He stood up and stretched his nose over toward Zach who gladly stuck out his finger one more time.

"Oooh, rancid! That's the foulest stench I've ever smelled in my life!" Graham coughed and waved his hand in front of his face. All of a sudden our entire table couldn't wait to smell Zach's disgusting finger. Even Diane, Heidi, and some of the other girls wanted a turn.

Finally, after we were all thoroughly grossed out, we started eating. "Zach, did you hear about my homer on Saturday?" Graham asked.

"Yeah. I wish I could have seen it," he answered.

"Don't worry, I've got plenty of them left," Graham said. "If you come to the next game I'll do it again."

"Me too," I added.

"Hi, sweetie—I mean, Raymond," Mom interrupted, setting down her lunch bag on the table between Graham and me. Then she squeezed in and sat down between us on the bench. "Isn't this fun? We get to eat together all week." The whole table looked at us. Teachers never eat with the kids. I don't know where they eat, but it's never with us. Suddenly all my friends were quiet.

"Please don't stop talking because of me," Mom said. We all just sat there in silence. "Zachary, how's your mother doing with that new baby brother of yours?"

"Um, fine, I guess," Zach said.

"And Graham, it's nice to see your hair is back to normal. It was such a shame hiding those precious red curls underneath all of that goop," she said, rubbing his curly hair.

"It's called gel. And I just ran out," Graham said.

"I agree with Raymond's mom—it looks more like goop than gel," Diane added. While Graham and Diane argued about the difference between gel and goop, I turned to my mom.

"Where did you eat yesterday?" I asked.

"In the teacher's lounge with the other teachers," she said. "But I thought it would be much more fun to sit out here with you and your friends."

Mom took out a plastic container and pulled off the lid. A terrible odor floated out and filled the air around our table. It was worse than Zach's finger. Everyone gasped.

"Oooh, what is that?" I asked, plugging my nose.

"It's the leftover liver and onions from dinner last night. And this," she said, opening another container, "is the sauerkraut from the night before." A stench even worse than the first one exploded into the air. "Would you like some, sweetie?"

"No way." I gagged.

A Stinky Lunch

"Hey, see you guys on the playground," Zach said. He jumped up and ran out the door.

"Yeah, me too," Graham said, picking up his mostly uneaten tray of food. "I've got to save the basketball court for us."

"Hold on, Graham," Mom said. "You haven't eaten any of those carrots." Graham looked at me as if to ask what he should do. I just shrugged my shoulders. Mom smiled and waited for him to eat them. Finally, Graham picked up a carrot stick, shoved it in his mouth, and ran out of the lunchroom.

"Well, that was fun, having lunch with you and your friends. I hope I didn't embarrass you," Mom said.

What could I say to that? "No, it was fun," I said. "But if you feel like you need to eat with the other teachers the rest of the week, I'll understand. I mean, you are technically a teacher."

"Not a chance," she answered, putting her arm around my shoulder. "I wouldn't miss eating with you for anything. Now run along and play with your friends. You don't need to wait for me to finish."

Just as I got up, Lizzy, who was sitting at a different table, came over and sat down right next to my mom. I could hear her talking as I made my way toward the door.

"Hi, Mrs. Knudson," Lizzy said. "I think you're the best substitute ever. And even though that stuff you're eating smells really bad, I don't even mind. I think it's a great lunch. . . ."

I shook my head and ran out to the basketball game, which had already started. "Hey, whose team am I on?" I yelled.

"Is your mom going to play too?" Zach laughed. With his broken finger, he was trying to shoot the basketball with his left hand.

"Come on, guys. What am I supposed to do?" I said. "She's my mom."

"It's all right. Just tell her not to talk to me about my 'precious red curls' anymore," Graham said. "Here, you're on our team." Graham threw me the ball. I dribbled and went for a layup. David jumped and threw his body into mine, knocking me to the ground. He usually didn't play basketball with us, but I guess it must have been my lucky day.

"Hey, that's a foul," Graham said.

"What's he going to do, tell on me to his mommy?" David sneered. "I'm just giving you a little taste of what it'd be like to play against the Pirates in the championship baseball game. Too bad you guys won't be there—unless you're watching from the bleachers."

"Oh, we'll be playing," Graham said. "I guarantee that. And this year, we're going to win." We needed a lot more wins if we were going to make it there, but Graham sounded like he really believed we could do it.

David just laughed. "Yeah, right," he said. "You guys probably won't even beat the Astros tonight, and they're in last place." He walked away before we could say anything to that.

With only a couple of minutes of recess left, we decided to quit the game. Zach stayed and shot a few more baskets, while Graham and I walked over toward the school doors.

"Man, I want to win that championship so bad," I said. "It's not even about the game. I just want to beat David."

"I know what you mean," Graham said. "But I've got a good feeling."

"I hope you're right," I said. The bell rang and we went back to class.

It was a long afternoon. Whenever my mom turned away, David would either hit my arm or lean over to tell me how bad our team was. I just wanted the day to end. Unfortunately, when the final bell did ring, my mom had another surprise for me. She asked me and David to stay and talk with her after the bell. I told Graham not to wait up.

"Raymond, I would like you to sit down for a few minutes and work with David on tonight's math assignment. David's doing just fine, but he could use a little help with the fractions." David and I looked at each other.

"But—" we both said at the same time.

"Don't worry, I spoke with David's mother when you were at recess, and she thought it was a great idea. I told her we would drive you home when you're done." With that, my mom pulled out two chairs at the back table for us and left us to work. "I'll be in the office for a bit," she added. Then she disappeared out the door.

"If you tell anyone about this, you're dead," David started. "I'm not stupid and I don't need your help." He was using the same mean words as always, but his voice was quieter, and instead of staring me in the eyes, he looked down at the ground as he talked.

"I know you're not stupid," I said. "Let's just get started."

We worked on fractions for the next thirty minutes. David asked me a lot of questions, and I explained things when he got something wrong. I could tell he needed the help. Luckily, I don't have any trouble with fractions. I actually kind of like them. When we finished going through the whole assignment, David closed his book and looked at me.

"Remember, don't tell anyone about this," he said.

"Don't worry, I won't," I said.

"Good. And don't think that this means you're not getting punched anymore."

Even after helping him with his math, nothing had changed. David stood up and walked over to his desk.

"By the way . . . um . . . thanks," he mumbled, not looking at me. Just then my mom appeared in the doorway.

"How did it go?" she asked.

"Good. We're done," I said. We all walked to the car. David and I sat silently in the back the whole way home.

What's the Signal?

COACH PARKER WANTED us to get to our game early that night. Since we had lost two games already, he said we needed to work extra hard to get back on track. He wanted to win the championship as much as we did, and if we didn't start playing better that wasn't going to happen. Once we all got there, Coach gathered us around home plate. "Okay, guys, listen up. I know we haven't worked on this yet this year, but we're going to start using some signals. Before you step up to the plate, you need to look over at me to see what I want you to do."

I wasn't sure what he meant. I mean, what would he want us to do besides hit the ball?

"Now, if I do this," he said, touching the brim of his hat and then sliding his hand across his chest, "it means you bunt on the next pitch. Does everyone understand?"

"Why don't you just yell 'bunt' in Spanish?" Carlos said.

"Great idea, *hermano*," Graham said, giving Carlos a high five. "We could learn the Spanish words for everything." We all looked at each other and nodded.

"Let's try to stick with our signals, okay?" said Coach. "If anyone on the other team understands Spanish, he'll know what we're doing."

I never thought of that. I guess that's why he's the coach.

"Okay, when I do this," Coach continued, sliding his right hand down his left arm and then sliding his left hand down his right arm, "it means swing hard, even if it's a bad pitch."

"Why would we swing if it's a bad pitch?" Zach asked.

"Well, because we want the runner on first base

to steal second base. If the batter swings, it will be more difficult for the catcher to catch the ball and throw the runner out."

Wow, I had never thought of that either. I hoped I would never have to swing at a bad pitch. There's no way I wanted to give up a strike just to make the base runner's life easier. Coach showed us another signal for when he wanted us not to swing, and then he said, "But if I clap after any signal, that means ignore whatever signal I gave you and just hit away."

I was getting really confused. "So if you give us a signal to bunt, but then you clap after the signal, we ignore it?" I asked.

"Right," he said. "It's just to confuse the other team, in case they're catching on to our signals. Now, since we've lost a couple of games, we need to get on a winning streak. And this year we're going to make it to the championships! Let's really work on getting the signals down in tonight's game."

We did a little infield practice as the Astros arrived one at a time. Then we let them take the field to warm up. After a few minutes the umpire showed up, put on his gear, and yelled, "Play ball!"

We were up to bat first. Coach Parker stood by third base. Luke's dad was coaching first base. Graham was batting first today. He walked up and pounded the plate with his bat. "Give me a good one!" he yelled out.

Graham let the first two pitches go by and complained when the umpire called them strikes. He stepped out of the box and looked at Coach, who was giving him a signal. Coach touched his hat, then slid his hand across his chest and clapped.

Graham looked confused. "One more time, please," he called down to Coach Parker. He gave him the signal one more time, and then said, "Let's go, bud. Let's get a hit." Graham looked over at us on the bench and mouthed, *"What?"*

"He said bunt," Zach yelled.

"No, he didn't, he clapped. Just hit like normal," Luke yelled.

"Hey, quiet, you guys," Luke's dad called over from first base. Coach Parker just shook his head.

Graham let the first one go by as a ball and then smacked the next one. He made it to first base. Carlos was up next.

As usual, his parents started yelling to him in Spanish. Coach gave him the signal to swing no matter what. The pitch was low and in the dirt. Carlos swung anyway, and Graham stole second base. The ball bounced behind the catcher, and Graham stole third base too. Carlos's parents were still yelling. I figured they were telling him to quit swinging at bad pitches. Someone needed to explain the whole signal thing to them. The next four pitches were all balls, and Carlos jogged down to first base.

I was up next. I looked over at Coach for my signal, hoping he would tell me to just hit away. He gave me the bunt sign. I waited a second or two. Maybe he would clap after the sign, but he didn't. I hate to bunt. First of all, I can't do it very well. And second, it's a stupid kind of hit. Who wants to hit a ball and have it roll five feet away? Baseball's about home runs and grand slams, not bunts. But

I followed Coach's directions and tried to bunt.

"Strike one!" the umpire yelled. I had missed the ball completely.

"Move in, everyone," their pitcher yelled. "He's bunting."

Coach whistled to me and gave me the signal to hit. I swung as hard as I could.

"Strike two!" the ump called out. Everyone on the other team moved back a little.

After two bad pitches, the Astros' pitcher threw the ball right down the middle. I felt a home run coming on. I swung as hard as I could and hit the ball. It bounced on the ground in front of the plate and rolled about halfway to the pitcher. It wasn't the home run I'd wanted, but I made it to first without getting out. Graham stayed on third. With the bases loaded, Luke stepped up to the plate and smacked a grand slam. Our entire team came out of the dugout and cheered Luke as he made it across home plate.

The rest of the game went well. After bunting when he was supposed to swing hard and not swinging at all when he was supposed to bunt, Graham finally figured out the signals. We didn't score any more runs, but we still won 4–2, thanks to Luke's grand slam homer.

I wondered if the nickname Luke the Puke would change now that he'd hit a grand slam and was the hero of the game. Unfortunately, the next morning at school he was still "the Puke" like always. I don't think anyone really meant anything mean by it—everyone had called him that for so long, it just seemed like his real name. Even his friends were saying things like "Great game, Puke Man!" and "Long live the Puke!" He didn't seem to mind it too much. Maybe he was as used to it as everyone else was.

Then at recess I saw Graham talking to Kelly and showing her all our signals. I couldn't believe it.

"Graham, can I talk to you?" I said, pulling him away from Kelly. She smiled and walked away quickly.

"Hey, what are you doing? Couldn't you see I was talking with Kelly?" he said.

"Yeah, I saw you. You were showing her our baseball signals. What if David saw you?"

"Wait a minute, *hermano*," Graham said, smiling. "I didn't show her our *team* signals. Those were my own signals."

"What are you talking about? I saw you give the 'don't swing' signal," I said.

"Well, I'm using the same signals, but they mean different things," he explained. "Since I didn't get to sit by her this week, I gave her some signals so I can talk to her from across the room. Like when I give the 'don't swing' signal, it means, 'Hi, Kelly, how's it going?' and the 'swing' signal means, 'What are you doing at recess?'"

"Are you serious?" I said. "That seems a little complicated."

"No way, it's going to be great," Graham said. "Just watch."

That afternoon in class I saw Graham giving Kelly signals from his desk. Kelly looked at him like he was crazy. My mom even asked him if he was all right.

Graham seemed sad after school as we walked down the school steps. "What's wrong?" I finally asked.

"Well, I was giving signals to Kelly all afternoon," Graham said.

"Yeah, I saw you. We all saw you," I said.

"Well, everyone but Kelly," he answered. "She didn't respond to any of them."

"What do you mean? How was she supposed to respond?"

Graham's eyebrows got all scrunched up, and he thought for a minute. "Hmm, you're right," he said. "I didn't give her any signals to answer me. She probably wanted to say something, but just didn't know how. I'll have to come up with some and show her tomorrow."

Graham smiled. "Thanks, *hermano*," he said to me. "You always know how to cheer me up." I smiled back and didn't say anything.

10

The Last Surprise

WHEN FRIDAY MORNING came, I was feeling great. It was finally the last day with my mom in class. I had made it through the first four days. Surely I could handle one more. But when I was brushing my teeth, my mom said something that scared me to death.

"Sweetie, I have to leave a little early today, so I can't drive you to school. But I do have one more surprise for you." My heart stopped. I couldn't handle another surprise from my mom—not after her last one.

"What is it?" I asked. I had to know. If I needed to prepare for this, I wanted to know as early as possible. "It's nothing about school, is it?"

"As a matter of fact, it *is* about school," she said.

"What is it? You've got to tell me," I begged.

"You'll find out soon enough," Mom said. "See you in class." She walked out the door and drove away without dropping even a hint about what was going on. Was Mrs. Gibson going to be out longer? Was Mom going to show our class my baby pictures? *She'd better not show the one of me crawling naked on my blanky,* I thought as I ate my scrambled eggs. I walked down to Graham's.

"Graham, something bad is going to happen," I told him the second he walked out the door.

"What are you talking about?" Graham said. "Everything's going great. We're getting closer to the playoffs, and today is the last day your mom will be eating lunch with us. I mean, no offense, I like your mom and all. It's just hard to talk about certain things when she's around."

"My mom is what's worrying me," I said. "She told me she has another surprise for me today. I don't know if I can take it. I've had enough surprises for one week." I was about to tell Graham about having to help David with his fractions, but since I promised David I wouldn't, I decided to keep it a secret. Plus, if he ever found out I told, I'm sure it would get me a huge slug on the arm.

"Relax," Graham said. "Surprises are usually good things. Maybe she bought you a present, or maybe your family's going to a movie tonight. Hey, if it's a movie, ask her if you can bring me. I really want to see *Mega-Brain vs. the Alien Slime*. I heard that—"

"Hold on," I said. "Look, we're not going to see *Mega-Brain* because—"

"That's all right," Graham interrupted. "It doesn't matter what we see. I like almost all movies. I even like the ones—"

"Would you forget about the movies?" I said, putting my hand over his mouth. "My mom said her surprise has something to do with school." Graham pulled my hand away.

"You don't think she's going to be our teacher

longer, do you?" he said. "What if she's our teacher forever? What if Mrs. Gibson decided not to come back?" A look of dread came over Graham's face.

"I don't know. That's what I'm trying to tell you," I said. "I don't think I could take another week of my mom being our teacher and everything else that goes with it."

"Me neither," Graham said. "Yesterday when I was talking to your mom at Mrs. Gibson's desk, I sneezed. Your mom grabbed a tissue, put it right on my nose, and told me to blow. Diane was standing behind her and watched the whole thing. I mean, even my own mom doesn't help me blow my nose anymore."

"Wow. Sorry about that," I said. I felt like she was my responsibility.

"It's okay. If Kelly had seen it, I would've been more upset. But I can handle Diane," Graham said.

We walked to school thinking about all the different awful surprises that might await us in our classroom. As we entered the room, everything looked normal so far. But Mom wasn't there yet, so I still couldn't relax.

"Hey, Raymond," Diane said, walking up behind us. Graham and I both spun around.

"You know, I'm kind of going to miss having your mom as our teacher. She's really nice."

"Yeah," Heidi added, jumping into the conversation. "I've never heard a teacher call a student 'sweetie' before."

We all laughed. "I've never seen a teacher help a kid blow his nose either," Diane said.

Graham's face turned red. "Hey, keep that quiet," he told her.

The bell rang and still no Mom. We all went to our desks and waited.

"So where's your mommy?" David said.

"I don't know. She had to go somewhere before school," I said. "She'll be here."

"She's probably at the store getting you some more diapers," he said, snickering.

Just then my mom walked through the door. "Sorry I'm late, everyone. I had to make one stop at the store." She walked up to Mrs. Gibson's desk and put down her purse and the folder of homework she had corrected. "Now, I know you miss Mrs. Gibson and school just isn't the same with a substitute. But I had a lot of fun teaching you this week. And to thank you for making me feel so welcome, I have a surprise."

My heart started beating fast, and I held my breath. What was it going to be?

"This afternoon, we are going to have a party," she said. "I have some soda and a piñata filled with candy in my car. So if we can get all of our work done early, we'll take the last hour of class to have our fiesta. How does that sound?"

Everyone cheered. Graham gave me a thumbs-up sign. I looked around at all the happy faces. *Maybe this week hasn't been so bad after all*, I thought.

We worked hard the whole day to make sure there was time for the party. I couldn't believe she'd gotten a piñata. Piñatas are the greatest invention ever. They combine two of my favorite things: baseball and candy. It's just like being up to bat, but instead of a ball, you get to swing at a cardboard animal filled with candy!

Finally, it was time. Mom had us all move our desks to the sides of the room to make a big open space in the middle. Then she told us the rules of the piñata. We each got three swings with the plastic bat, and then it was someone else's turn. Mom had a big sombrero that she bought when she and my dad went on a trip to Mexico. She put it on my head and said, "Raymond, you get to go first. And when you're done, you get to choose who goes next by putting the sombrero on his or her head."

The piñata hung from a rope that was tied to the end of a long broom handle. Mom stood on a chair and held out the broom handle, dangling the donkey-shaped piñata in the middle of the open space. "Everyone else stand back here by the wall. We don't want anyone to get hit," she said.

Mom blindfolded me and handed me a stick.

"Whenever you're ready, go ahead and swing."

I pulled the bat back and swung as hard as I could. I missed the piñata and fell down.

"That's how you play baseball too," David yelled out, laughing.

"David," Mom said sternly. "That was uncalled for, especially during a fiesta. If you want a turn at the piñata, you have to be nice."

I swung again and hit the bottom of the piñata, but it didn't break.

"Strike two." David laughed again. I hated that guy. I wanted to say something like, "I didn't know you could count to two—my math lessons must be working." But I didn't say anything.

My third swing hit the piñata straight on, but it didn't break.

"Okay, good job, Raymond," Mom said. "Now pick someone to go next." I pulled off the blindfold and looked around at all the waving hands. I knew exactly who I was going to pick. David tried to grab the hat as I walked down the line of kids, but I went straight to Heidi and put the sombrero on her head. Mom put the blindfold over her eyes and guided her to the middle of the room. Heidi hit the piñata twice, but it didn't break. Then she put the sombrero on Diane, who also hit it, but still no candy fell. Suzy Rivera was next. She was the smallest girl in our class, but she really smacked the piñata hard. On her first swing she made a small hole in it, and two pieces of candy fell out.

"Please leave the candy on the floor until she's done hitting," my mom said. David didn't listen and ran out to get the candy. Just then Suzy swung again. This time she missed the piñata and hit David in the arm.

"Ouch!" he yelped, grabbing his arm.

"Oh, dear!" Mom yelled, jumping down from her chair. "Are you all right?"

"I'm fine," David said quickly. "It doesn't hurt." He walked back to his spot.

"Everyone, please stay back until after the third swing," my mom said. "That was a good example of what will happen if we don't follow the rules."

"I would never run out there early," Lizzy said. "And I think this is a great party, Mrs. Knudson."

"Thank you, Lizzy. I appreciate your obeying the rules." I couldn't believe Mom didn't see

OUCH!

through Lizzy's kiss-up-ness. Suzy got to redo her final swing, and then we all ran out to get the two pieces of candy. Zach made it there first and snatched up both pieces.

Suzy felt bad for hitting David, so she put the sombrero on his head.

"Now you guys will see what a real hitter can do. Get ready for the candy," he said. Mom put the blindfold on him and got back up on her chair. I could tell by the way she was moving the piñata that she was going to make it hard for David. His first swing missed completely.

"Nice hit, slugger," Graham called out.

Mom gave him a stern look. "Graham—"

"Sorry," Graham said, hoping to avoid a lecture on proper fiesta behavior.

"Just wait," David yelled back. He swung again, barely touching the edge of the piñata. Then he just started swinging wildly. My mom moved the piñata away after about his tenth swing.

"Your turn is over, David. Time for someone else to have a try." David ripped off the blindfold and the sombrero, dropped them on the floor, and stomped back to his place.

"Thanks for all the candy," Diane said. Everyone laughed.

I looked over at David and felt a little sad for him. Part of me was happy he missed the piñata, but part of me wished he could have broken it open. *Maybe he's so mean because people expect him to be mean*, I thought. *Maybe if he broke the piñata open and everyone cheered for him, he would act a little differently.* "Hey, David," I called over to him. "If you had hit the piñata, it definitely would have exploded. Those were some really hard swings."

"Way harder than yours," he shot back.

Oh, well, so much for niceness, I thought. Mom gave me one of those "I'm proud of you" smiles. I smiled back.

"Okay, Graham, why don't you go next?" Mom said. Graham ran out excitedly and threw on the blindfold. He swung hard and knocked an ear off the donkey. Unfortunately, no candy fell out. He missed his next two swings. I think my mom was trying to make it hard so everyone would get a chance. I don't think Graham cared if he broke the piñata—all he cared about was putting the sombrero on Kelly. He took off the blindfold and walked straight over to her.

"This is for you, my lovely señorita," he said, putting the sombrero on her head. Kelly walked up and, on her first swing, broke the piñata completely in two, spilling candy all over the floor. No one waited for any more swings. We all rushed in and grabbed as much candy as we could.

As we scrambled around on the floor, Mom poured soda into paper cups and set out some cookies on the table in the back. We ate candy and cookies until the end-of-school bell rang.

"Before you leave, let's put the desks back where they belong and make sure everything on the floor is picked up," Mom said. Everyone hurried to get the room looking normal again and then left. Graham and I stayed after and helped my mom clean up some of the pieces of piñata that were still on the floor. It was a great ending to a crazy week.

11

Pictures and Dorkwads

MRS. GIBSON RETURNED the next week, and everything was back to normal. Lizzy was back to sucking up to Mrs. Gibson. Graham was back to throwing out his vegetables. And David was back to moving his desk up by Mrs. Gibson's for doing something bad.

On Wednesday, Mr. Worley announced that class pictures would be passed out at the end of the day. I looked over at Graham. He was wiggling around in his seat and quietly clapping his hands underneath his desk. Later that day at lunch recess, Graham said, "After school I'm going to trade pictures with Kelly. Are you going to get one from Heidi?"

"I don't know," I answered.

Graham looked at me like I was crazy. "What do you mean you don't know?"

"I mean, I don't have a wallet like you. And besides, what if she doesn't want to give me one or doesn't want mine?"

Graham shook his head like he couldn't believe what he was hearing. "Who cares?" he said. "When you ask someone for their picture, there's no way they would say no. That would just be rude."

"I don't know, we'll see," I said.

Just before school ended, Mrs. Gibson passed out the pictures. We all opened them to see how we looked. Even with my girl shirt, I thought mine looked pretty good. Lizzy took out her biggest picture, the one that your mom usually hangs on the wall at home. She brought it to Mrs. Gibson.

"Here, this is for you," Lizzy said, setting the photo on Mrs. Gibson's desk.

"That's very sweet of you, Lizzy. But I couldn't take this big picture—your parents would be so sad." Lizzy looked heartbroken.

"How about this," Mrs. Gibson quickly added.

"Why don't you take them home and ask your mother if she could spare one of these small pictures, and you can bring it to me tomorrow?" Now Lizzy looked thrilled.

The final bell rang, and we all stormed the door—except Graham. He ran toward the back of the class to the tables where we do our art projects. Grabbing a pair of scissors, he carefully cut out one of the eight wallet-size photos from his sheet.

"Come on, man," I said.

"Almost done," Graham answered. Then he threw the scissors back into the plastic tray with the other art stuff, and we ran out the door.

Once outside, Graham spied Kelly by the crosswalk.

"I'll be back," he told me. He sprinted to catch up with her. His backpack swung around and hit Diane as he passed by.

"Hey, watch it!" Diane shouted. She turned around and asked me, "What's the deal with Graham?" Diane and Heidi waited for me to catch up with them.

"He's trying to trade pictures with Kelly," I said. Then I thought, *This is my chance.* I could ask both Diane and Heidi if they wanted to trade pictures. Then it wouldn't look like I was just trying to get Heidi's picture.

"So do you guys want to trade pictures?" I asked.

"No," Diane said. "I only bought the class picture and the big one."

"I bought the whole package, so I have eight of the small wallet pictures," Heidi said. "But after I give one to my grandparents, Diane, the mailman, and some of my neighbors, I don't think I'll have any extras."

I stood there not knowing what to think. *Even the mailman gets one before me?* Then I saw a smile start to spread onto Heidi's face.

"I'm just kidding! Sure, let's trade," she said. Just then Graham made it back.

"She's going to cut one out at home and bring it to me tomorrow," he proudly informed us. We all walked home together laughing about what the mailman would think if we asked him to trade pictures.

Another week passed, and it was like Mrs. Gibson had never even been gone. The best part was that during those two weeks, we won three more games and only lost one. Now we were tied with the Tigers for second place. David's team still hadn't lost once.

On Tuesday we had to play a tiebreaker game against the Tigers. The winner would play the Pirates on Saturday in the championship game. I was so nervous I struck out three times. I wanted to hit the ball so badly I was swinging at everything, even when coach gave me the "don't swing" signal.

Fortunately for us, everyone else on our team was playing great. Graham was hitting like crazy, and Kevin got a home run. It was a close game, but we ended up winning by one run. Our entire team ran out, jumped around, and cheered like we had just won the World Series. We had made it! Saturday we would be in the championships.

Thanks to Graham, the championship game was the talk of our class for the rest of the week. He had invited everyone who wasn't playing to come and watch. David and Brian were promising a win for the Pirates. Graham and I walked home on Friday with a group of kids and couldn't stop talking about it.

"We're definitely coming to the game," Diane said.

"Yeah, we wouldn't miss it," Heidi added. I was nervous about having everyone there to watch us play.

"Well, if you have something else going on, it's okay if you can't come," I said.

"What?" Graham said. "Of course, you're all coming. We need all the fans we can get. It's time that David and those stupid Pirates go down."

"I know. I'm sick of that guy bragging about how they're going to destroy your team," Diane said.

"Even though I won't be able to play, I'll be there," Zach said. "I wouldn't miss this game for anything." His finger was still bandaged up.

"Well, I can't wait for David to get up to bat," Graham said. "I've been working on my insults for him."

Graham and I played a little catch that afternoon, but I went home early to make sure I got enough rest for the game. I went to bed right after dinner, but I had a hard time sleeping. All I could think about was the first game this season when David struck me out. His crazy laugh kept echoing in my brain.

When morning came I could smell bacon cooking. I jumped up, put on my uniform, and ran into the kitchen. I loved bacon and eggs, and it seemed like the perfect breakfast for an athlete.

"Hey, slugger," my dad said. He was sitting at the kitchen table reading the paper. "Ready for the big game?"

"Yeah, I guess so."

"Raymond, would you please go tell your sister that breakfast is ready?" Mom said. I hated that job, especially on Saturdays when Geri wanted to sleep in. She was extra grouchy on the weekends.

I huffed upstairs, knocked on Geri's door, and yelled, "Hey, Geri, get up! We're having breakfast."

"Go away, dorkwad," she yelled back.

"Mom said to come down," I replied. "She's making waffles with strawberries and whipped cream." That was her favorite. I knew it would get her downstairs even if it was a lie.

"Fine, I'll be right there," she growled. I returned to the table where Mom and Dad were already seated and waiting to start. Geri followed close behind.

"Hey, what's this? Raymond said we were having strawberry waffles with whipped cream," Geri said, looking at the plate of scrambled eggs and bacon.

"She wasn't going to come down otherwise," I said.

"Raymond, we don't lie in this house," Mom said. "I'm sure your sister would have come anyway." Geri smiled and made a face at me.

"Yeah, well, she lied too," I said.

"How did I lie?" Geri snapped back.

"You called me a dorkwad."

"That's not a lie. You *are* a dorkwad."

"Can we just have a nice meal together without the bickering, please?" Mom said. "Is that too much to ask?"

"No," I said. "Thanks for making breakfast."

"What is a dorkwad, anyway?" Dad asked. Mom gave him a stern look.

After breakfast, I called Graham to see if he was as excited as I was. He was already in his uniform too. We decided we would go to the ballpark early as usual. I asked my mom if she would drive us.

"Sure, sweetie," she said. "How early do you want to go?"

"We want to go now!" I said.

"But you're an hour and a half early."

"So what? We want to get there before anyone else, to get mentally prepared. You know, to smell the grass and kick up the dirt and sit on the bench

silently, thinking about the true meaning of baseball and all that kind of stuff, before anyone else
shows up." Mom looked at me really strangely.

"Well, if that's what you two want, get in the
car and I'll take you."

I ran out to the car and waited while Mom
searched for her purse. When we got to Graham's
house, he was on the curb. He had his bat in one
hand and a ball in the other. His baseball glove
was pulled over the end of the bat.

"Good morning, Graham," Mom said. She
clenched her teeth when Graham's bat hit the side
of the car as he climbed in.

"Hi, Mrs. Knudson," he answered. Then he
turned to me. "We are going to crush the Pirates."

"I hope so," I replied. "Just once, I'd like to beat
David at baseball, or anything else for that matter. If we win, it will be the greatest moment of
my life."

"Oh, we're going to win," Graham said. "I promised Kelly we would. I told her I was dedicating the
game to her."

"Wow, what did she say?" I asked.

"She didn't really say anything," Graham said. "She must have been speechless. I mean, what can you say when someone dedicates something as massive as the championship game to you?"

"I don't know—nothing, I guess."

We finally got to the baseball field. Graham's bat smacked the car window as he got out. Mom clenched her teeth again. "We'll see you boys in a little while," she said.

"Bye, Mom," I called back as we ran to the field.

We played catch for a few minutes. Then we sat down in the dugout and quietly stared at the field.

"This is where it's all going to take place, *hermano*," Graham said.

"Yep. The biggest moment of our lives. In just one more hour, I'll be out there pitching to David," I said. "He'll be laughing and teasing me, and I won't even care. Today, I'll have the last laugh."

"That's right," Graham said. "This is the year of the Giants."

As we sat there staring out at the field, a terrible, familiar sound broke our silence.

"Hey, losers. Stuck on the bench already? You two are probably used to that." I knew who it was without even turning around. The crazy laugh that followed confirmed my suspicions.

"We'll see who the loser is!" Graham yelled back at David, who was passing by the back of our dugout on his way to the other side of the field. David's team followed close behind him. They were all here early.

"What are they doing here already?" I asked Graham.

"I don't know," he said. "Warming up, I guess."

After running a lap around the field, they all hurried to their positions while their coach hit balls to them.

"Take it to first!" the coach yelled, hitting a grounder to the third baseman. The kid picked it up and burned it over to first. "You've got to be quicker than that, Jackson!"

"How could you get any quicker than that?" I

said to Graham quietly. I didn't want their coach to hear me. Even though we weren't on his team, I still felt a little scared of him.

"He's just trying to intimidate us," Graham said.

"What's going on out there?" the coach screamed to an outfielder. "Give me two laps!"

"Sorry!" the kid called back, starting to jog.

"Pick up the pace. My grandmother can run faster than that!" the coach added.

I figured his grandma must have been pretty old, since he didn't look too young himself. The longer we sat there watching the Pirates warm up and listening to their coach scream, the happier we were to be on Coach Parker's team.

Finally our team showed up. We took the field, and Coach hit balls to us. Slowly, the crowd of parents and friends arrived and filled the small bleachers on both sides of the field. Luke's mom opened the snack bar.

Graham elbowed me in the ribs. "Hey, look who's here!" He was pointing to the parking lot.

"No way," I said. It was Coach Cunningham from the Marlins, the defending champs in the majors. Two of his players were with him. I straightened my hat and tucked in my jersey. I wanted to make sure I looked like a baseball player.

"Five minutes, coach," the umpire called out to Coach Parker.

"All right, everyone, bring it in," Coach yelled. We all ran and huddled up in a circle just outside our dugout.

"Okay, team," he started. "This is what we worked all season for. Let's play our hardest and win the championship! Giants, on the count of three." We all put our hands in the middle and yelled, *"One, two, three, Giants!"*

"Play ball!" the umpire announced.

12

The Big Game

"**ALL RIGHT, TEAM,** grab your gloves and get out on the field. The Pirates are up first," Coach said. We all ran onto the field. I pitched a few warm-up throws to Graham. I was nervous, but I was ready for this game.

The Pirates' first batter stepped up. Graham gave me a couple of signals. I shook my head until he got to the "fastball" signal. As soon as I let go of the ball, I knew it was a bad pitch. The batter tried to jump back, but he didn't make it in time. The ball hit him in the arm. He threw his bat to the ground and walked to first base, giving me an evil glare the whole way.

"It's all right, bud. Shake it off," Coach yelled. I

looked over at the crowd. I saw my mom, Dad, and Geri sitting by my grandma and Gramps on the top row of the bleachers. My grandma had even brought her special homemade caramel corn. My mom waved. Sitting right in front of them were Diane, Heidi, and Kelly. I hadn't thought Kelly would really come. She had seemed like she was kind of getting sick of Graham. But maybe dedicating the game to her really *was* a good idea.

"Nice pitch, Raymond," Dad called out to me. "He was too close to the plate."

I didn't think he was too close—I just threw a bad pitch. Brian's mom seemed to agree with me.

"It wasn't a nice pitch!" she told Dad.

"It was a beautiful pitch!" he answered.

"Listen to the umpire. It was a bad throw," Brian's mom called back.

Dad waited a few seconds and then said in a quiet but firm voice, "Good pitch." Geri, looking embarrassed, moved down two rows in the bleachers.

The next batter hit it to third base, but both

runners were safe. I walked the next batter, and now the bases were loaded. David was up to bat. Graham could tell I was nervous and ran out to the pitcher's mound.

"Hey, don't worry about David. He's nothing. You just throw good pitches, and I'll take care of the rest," Graham said. He walked slowly back to his position behind home plate.

David walked up and hit the plate with his bat. "Let's see what you've got, wimp!" he yelled.

"Give him the special," Graham called out to me.

"Oooh, the special. I'm really scared," David said, looking at Graham.

"Forget the special. How about the piñata—I know he can't hit that." Graham laughed.

"You're gonna pay for that!" David said, pounding the plate even harder.

"Let's play ball, boys," the ump called out.

I started my windup and could hear Graham still talking.

"Swing, don't swing, swing, don't swing," Graham said over and over.

"Strike one," the ump yelled. David didn't even swing.

"Oh, was that too fast for you? Give him a slow one, that was too fast," Graham called out.

The next pitch was high, but David swung as hard as he could and missed.

"Now, David," Graham said. "Why would you swing at such a high pitch? I'll bet this next one is high, too, and you'll swing at it. Hey, Raymond, how about another high one for the big guy?"

"Shut up!" David screamed.

"Okay, I'll be very, very, very quiet. You won't even know I'm here. I'll just catch this next high pitch without saying a word." The next pitch was my best so far. It was right down the middle. David looked like he was about to swing, but at the last minute he didn't.

"Strike three, batter's out!" the ump yelled.

"You're dead!" David growled to Graham as he stomped back to the dugout.

That was exactly what I needed. Our crowd was cheering, and I felt better than ever. I struck out the next batter, and we got the next guy out at first.

The Giants all ran to the dugout and gathered around Coach.

"Okay, here's the batting order," he said. "We're starting with Carlos, then Graham, Raymond, and Luke. The rest of you guys, be ready. And everyone cheer your teammates." Then he jogged over to third base. Luke's dad was standing by first. I looked up at the bleachers. Diane and Gramps were cheering and giving each other high fives. Heidi gave me a smile and a little wave.

Now the other team was in position on the field.

"Hey, look," I said. "David's not pitching."

"No way!" Graham said. "This is going to be easier than I thought."

I looked at the other dugout and saw David sitting on the bench, not looking very happy. Suddenly, a whole new level of confidence filled my body.

Carlos walked up to the plate. Coach gave him

a "swing away" signal, and on the very first pitch, he hit a line drive into right field. It hit the ground and then bounced back to the fence. Carlos made it to second base for a double. We all cheered.

Graham walked confidently to the plate. He looked at Coach Parker, who gave him the "swing away" signal too. Graham pointed over at Kelly and yelled, "This one's for you!" Kelly turned away like she was pretending not to hear.

"What?" came a voice from the crowd. "This one's for *me*?" It was Gramps. He must have thought Graham was talking to him, since he was sitting right behind Kelly.

Graham looked over at the bleachers. "No, I said it's for—"

"Strike one!" the umpire yelled. Graham wasn't paying attention, and the pitcher had thrown a perfect pitch right down the middle. Now Graham was mad. He dug his feet into the dirt.

"Give me another one like that if you dare!" he growled.

"Strike two!" yelled the ump after another near-perfect pitch.

"That was outside!" Graham complained. The next pitch was high, but Graham swung anyway.

"Strike three, batter's out!" Graham hit the ground with his bat and kicked up some dirt.

"It's all right, bud," Coach called from third base. "You'll get it next time." Graham stomped back to the dugout and pulled off the batting helmet. His face was red and his hair was sticking up like flames.

"Don't worry, *hermano*," I said. "That second pitch really was outside." He didn't answer. He just sat down at the end of the bench.

"Hey, partner," Gramps yelled down to Graham. "Next time you dedicate something to me, let's make it a hit!" Then he laughed and slapped himself on the knee. Grandma whapped Gramps with her purse.

Now it was my turn to bat. I knew I could get a hit off this guy. I pulled the bat back and waited for the perfect pitch. The first two throws were balls.

"Give it a ride, son!" Dad cheered. "A home run gets you five dollars from Gramps!"

"What?" Gramps said.

The next ball was perfect. I hit it hard to the shortstop, and it went through his legs. The Pirates' coach screamed, and I was safe at first. Carlos also ran home and scored our first run. I looked over to see if Heidi had seen my hit. She and Diane were turned around talking to my grandpa. At least my dad saw. He and my mom were standing up and cheering.

Luke was up next. He hit the ball to the second baseman, who picked it up and stepped on the base to get me out. Our next batter struck out. The first inning was over, and it was 1–0 for us.

The next few innings were tough. The Pirates clobbered us in the second inning and scored four runs. Coach pulled us all together and gave us a pep talk.

"This is it, men," he said. "I've coached most of you for three years now. You've worked hard, and you deserve to win this championship. But it's up to you to step up and play your best. Luke, remember that home run you hit a couple of games ago?" Luke nodded his head. "Let's get out there and do it again. You're up first. Keep your eye on the ball and hit it hard. That goes for the rest of you too. Let's give it all we've got. Now get your hands in here. On the count of three, in your loudest Giants voices, I want to hear you scream, 'Hit, run, score!'"

We all huddled up with our hands in the middle.

"*Hit, run, score!*" we screamed. The Pirates looked jealous of how pumped we were.

Luke got up to the plate and smacked the ball on his first swing. He didn't get a home run, but he did get a double.

"Nice hit, Puke Man!" our bench cheered. Luke smiled and gave us a thumbs-up.

We were so pumped up we couldn't sit down. Our entire team was at the fence screaming, and everyone started hitting the ball. The Pirates' coach finally pulled out their pitcher and put David on the mound. But the damage was already done. By the end of the inning, not only were we back in the game, we were up by two runs.

You're Out!

IT WAS DOWN to the last inning.

The last few innings had been really intense. No one had scored any runs at all. Every time we hit the ball they were able to get us out, and we did the same to them. Graham even threw off his catcher's mask, ran all the way to the Pirates' dugout, and dove to catch a foul ball. Both teams were playing like we were in the real World Series.

Now the Pirates were up. We were ahead 6–4. All we needed to do was hold the Pirates to one run or less and we would not have to bat again. We would win the game.

Kevin was pitching for us now. I took his place

in center field. The first batter hit the ball over second base and straight to me. I dove to catch it, but missed. Luke ran over from left field and picked up the ball.

Kevin struck out the next two batters and then walked one. There were two men on base when David stepped up to the plate. He looked serious. There was no making fun of our pitcher or any other trash talking. We were one out away from winning the championship.

The first pitch was inside. It almost hit David, but he didn't even flinch. The next was in the dirt. Again, David just watched it go by. He was waiting for the perfect pitch. Kevin's next throw was exactly what David was waiting for and he smacked it. I followed the ball with my eyes. It was coming straight toward me. But instead of coming down, it kept on sailing higher and farther. I ran back to the fence, but knew in an instant that it was gone, a home run. David punched his fists into the air as he jogged around the bases. I felt my heart sink. We were now losing by one run. Kevin struck the next batter out, and we all ran into the dugout.

Coach Parker stood in front of our bench. "You all know what we need to do," he said simply. "Let's do it." Then he walked down to third base. We were back to the beginning of our lineup. It would be Carlos, then Graham, and then me.

The first three pitches were balls. Coach gave the "don't swing" signal for the next pitch. Carlos stood there and watched the next pitch hit the ground in front of the plate.

"Ball four. Take your base," the umpire shouted. Carlos ran to first.

"Go get 'em, *hermano*," I said to Graham.

He grabbed his bat and walked up to the fence in front of the crowd. "Okay, this one is *really* for you," he said, pointing to Kelly. Gramps opened his mouth and was about to say something.

"Not you," Graham said, stopping him before he could say anything. "This is for Kelly."

Diane and Heidi and most of the crowd started laughing. Kelly looked really embarrassed. Graham didn't care. He walked up to the plate and yelled, "Come on, wimp. Throw the ball!"

No one ever called David a wimp. His face was red as he started his windup. He threw the ball straight at Graham, who just stood there with a smile and didn't move. The ball hit him in the leg. Now Graham's face turned red. I could tell he was in some serious pain and wanted to scream. Instead he just kept that stupid smile on his face and gently set the bat down on the ground. He gave two thumbs up to the crowd, who all cheered him down to first base.

Now David was *really* mad, and unfortunately, I was up next. This would probably be my last time up to bat in Little League. We were so close to winning the game and finally beating David. I just had to hit the ball.

Carlos and Graham were leading off their bases, getting ready to steal. Coach gave me the sign to swing no matter what. The first pitch was almost in the dirt, but I swung anyway and missed. Carlos and Graham both ran. The catcher threw the ball to third base to get Carlos out, but it went over the third baseman's head. Carlos kept running and slid home for the tying run. Graham made it to second base safely.

"You're going down," David yelled at me.

The next pitch almost hit me in the head. I hurled myself to the ground to avoid getting killed. Suddenly, it felt like the first game of the season again. The next pitch was a strike, but I didn't swing.

I stepped away from the plate and took a deep breath. I glanced over at Heidi and Diane. They were both smiling at me. Heidi had her fingers crossed. My mom had her hands over her eyes, like she was too nervous to watch. Gramps was stuffing a handful of caramel corn into his mouth.

This is it, I thought. *I can do this. My friends are here, my family is here, even my grandma and caramel-covered Gramps. I'm ready.* I stepped back up to the plate.

David said something, but I didn't pay attention. Then he wound up and threw the fastest pitch I had ever seen. I didn't have any time to decide if it was a strike or a ball, so I just swung as hard as I could. I felt the ball hit my bat and send vibrations up my arms.

"Run, run!" I heard everyone shout. I dropped the bat and ran to first as the ball sailed over the shortstop's head. The left fielder picked it up and threw it to third base, trying to get Graham out. Fortunately, Graham slid and was safe.

I couldn't believe it. I'd finally gotten a hit off David! Our crowd stood up and cheered. I hoped Coach Cunningham had seen my hit.

"Time-out," the Pirates' coach yelled. He walked out and had a little chat with David.

Graham yelled "Way to go, *hermano*!" from third base. Luke's dad whispered to me, telling me to take a big lead and to try to steal second base on the first pitch. I took about five steps off the base.

"Way to go, Raymond!" I heard someone call out from the stands. I looked over to see if it was Heidi.

Diane and Heidi were trying to say something

to me. *Probably trying to tell me I did a great job*, I thought. Now more people were telling me something . . . and pointing. Luke's dad was yelling something too, but with everyone screaming it just got all jumbled up. I turned to see what they were pointing at, only to see David running straight for me with the ball. I turned to run back to first, but it was too late. David had tagged me. "You're out," he shouted.

David stood there laughing in my face. The crowd went silent. I looked up at David and wanted to say something, but what could I say? I felt like I was going to die. But as I stared into David's mean black eyes, I caught a glimpse of something behind him. It was Graham, and he was heading home from third base. David and everyone else had forgotten all about him. Now it was the other team's crowd that was screaming. My smile must have given it away, because David quickly turned around. With Graham almost to the plate, David threw the ball to the catcher. The sound of the ball hitting the catcher's mitt echoed through the park just as Graham slid, raising a cloud of dirt.

All eyes were on the umpire. It seemed like time stood still as we waited for the call.

"Safe!" he finally shouted.

Our entire team ran out of the dugout and jumped around like crazy. We ran over to Graham, who was still on the ground at home plate. We tried to pick him up and put him on our shoulders, but we all fell down, so we just kept jumping around instead. We gave the other team a cheer, and both teams met at home plate to shake hands. I saw David coming toward me. I turned quickly and walked away to shake someone else's hand. The last thing I wanted was a slug on the arm to ruin this moment. But I wasn't quick enough.

"Hey, Raymond." I turned.

He was standing there with his hand stretched out toward me. "Good game," he said. I was waiting for the punch line or maybe just the punch, but it never came. I looked at his hand and then up at his face. He was serious.

I reached out and shook his hand. "Yeah, good game," I answered. Then we both moved on and shook hands with everyone else.

The crowd came running onto the field. I gave my mom and dad hugs. Grandma gave me a wet kiss, and Gramps pulled off my hat and rubbed my hair like he was trying to rub it all off. Even Geri gave me a little, friendly sneer. Then Coach brought us together with our parents and told us how proud he was of us and what a great season we'd had. He said something nice about each player. He seemed as happy as we were. My dad called out, "Let's hear it for Coach Parker!" All the parents and players gave Coach a cheer.

Coach gathered us in close. "How about one last cheer for the Giants, the new Little League champs!" We all stuck our hands in the circle. "Okay, 'we're number one'—on three." Coach counted and we screamed at the top of our lungs, *"We're number one!"* Then we all threw our hats into the air.

"And before you leave," Coach announced, "let's thank Zach's parents, who have volunteered to host a Giants' pool party at their house next Saturday." We all cheered again.

Coach Cunningham approached our team as we were still huddled up.

"Congratulations, Giants," he said. He put one hand on my shoulder as he leaned in to shake Coach Parker's hand. "I hope to see some of you in Marlins uniforms next season." Graham and I looked at each other, hoping he meant us.

Just then Diane, Heidi, and Kelly walked up to me and Graham. "Great game, you guys," Kelly said. "I've got to go. I'll see you on Monday, Graham." Then she walked away. Graham followed her with his eyes like he was in a trance.

"Hey, I finally came to a game that you won," Diane joked. She slapped Graham on the back and jolted him out of his zombie state.

"Uh, thanks," Graham said.

"It doesn't get much better than this," I said. Just then Gramps interrupted us.

"Hey, slugger, why don't I treat you and your friends to some championship ice cream?"

"Sure!" I said. Graham, Heidi, and Diane all nodded their heads.

"Who wants to race the champs to the car?" Graham announced. Before he could start running, Diane grabbed him and pulled him to the ground, then ran.

"Who's the champ now?" she called back to the rest of us.

"No fair," Graham cried from the ground. But she was long gone.

Just as I was about to run, Heidi grabbed my shoulder. "Wait, Raymond," she said. "I almost forgot to give this to you." She reached into her pocket and pulled out a wallet-size picture of her and handed it to me.

Graham got up and came over to see what was going on. When I turned the picture over, I saw she had written her name on it. Not only that, but she drew a little heart right next to it!

I looked up to say thanks, but she was already running to the car.

Graham and I looked at each other and smiled. We gave one more glance at the empty baseball field and slowly walked to the car. Somehow, even though we were just beaten by two girls, we still felt like champions.